A BEAR CALLED

EUSTON

THE EVIL TWIN

Published in 2009 by Prion
An imprint of the Carlton Publishing Group
20 Mortimer Street
London W1T 3JW

10987654321

A CIP catalogue record for this book is available from the British
Library.

ISBN 978 1 85375 690 0

Illustrations by Peter Liddiard

Printed in the UK

A BEAR CALLED
EUSTON
THE EVIL TWIN

Keillor Robertson

PRION

Contents

Chapter 1

Please Watch Yourself When In The Vicinity Of This Bear

Mr and Mrs Wood first met Euston Bear at Euston railway station.

Yes! Do you see? That's why they gave him the name Euston!

That and the fact that they were a dull, highly unimaginative, intellectually challenged couple who couldn't help reacting to the slightest stimulus put in front of them.

It was a bit like calling your child Brooklyn.

Mr and Mrs Wood toyed with other names first.

"We could call him Railway Bear!" said Mr Wood.

"Or Station Bear!" suggested Mrs Wood.

"I've got a better idea!" piped up the little bear. "Why don't you just ask me what my ****ing name is!"

"I've got it!" said Mr Wood noticing a large sign over the station platform. "Let's call him Virgin Express Bear!"

"I particularly object to that one! It makes me sound like some kind of specialist delivery service for the likes of this big ponce," said the bear, indicating Mr Wood with an angry gesture of his paw.

In the end, Mr and Mrs Wood decided Euston was the best, least weird name for the little fellow. So Euston Bear it was! Or, to give him his full name, Euston Just-Opposite-

Sock-Shop-Next-To-The-Pool-Of-Urine-By-The-Top-Of-The-Escalators Bear.

Mr and Mrs Wood had been so busy coming up with names for the bear that they had completely failed to notice something. Ever since they had met him, Euston had been attempting to mug the pair of them. So far, however, he had been unsuccessful in this enterprise. Essentially if you introduce yourself to someone with the words, "'Ey, mister, hand over your wallet or you're a dead man!" only to receive the response, "Oh look, darling. Isn't he sweet?" you are probably not going to enjoy a successful day's mugging.

Euston had, in fact, spent the whole morning trying to mug as many of the people on the station concourse as he possibly could. He was, of course, at a slight disadvantage in doing this. He was a small, soft, furry, two-and-a-half-feet-tall teddy bear while the people at the station comprised several thousand rather large individuals wearing a range of pointy shoes and heavy boots. The effect did not so much resemble a mass mugging by a small bear as a rough and rather painful, three-hour long, thousand-a-side game of football using a small, grey, furry ball. This was then followed for good measure by several minutes light polishing of the concourse floor with a small, grey, furry duster.

By the time he met the Woods, Euston was looking somewhat the worse for wear. He was grey, he was battered and he was covered in the accumulated detritus of the station concourse floor.

"I like your outfit," said Mrs Wood looking the little bear over. "Is that sweater you're wearing Angora?"

Euston explained that he was not currently wearing "no jumper nor nuffink."

He then went on to demonstrate that he was in fact completely naked in a manner that left Mrs Wood with no room for further doubt.

The Angora sweater effect she had noted was, he told her, the same as anyone would have been wearing if a thousand commuters had just used them to brush the floor of a large London station.

"But what about those pink rubbery epaulettes on your shoulders?" asked Mrs Wood.

"You don't want to know what they are, missus," said Euston. "Now for the last time, are you going to hand over your cash or what?"

"Yes," announced Mr Wood musing on the idea once again. "I think Euston is a capital name for the little chap."

"Oh for f…." said Euston. This attempted mugging was going even less well than when he had tried to rob a dead tramp half an hour earlier.

"I'll tell you what!" said Mr Wood, brightly. "Why don't we take the little bear home with us?"

"Hey!" said Euston. "I know your game!"

"I beg your pardon?" said Mr Wood.

"I'm not saying nothing," said Euston, "but you should know home visits are twenty quid extra."

"What are you talking about?" asked Mrs Wood.

"Your husband, missus," replied Euston. "Is he some kind of bear fiddler or what?"

"A bear fiddler?" asked Mrs Wood.

"You know what I'm talking about, lady," said Euston. "A bear botherer. A grizzly groper. A polar poker. A panda pimp. A Rupert rogerer. A man with an unnatural interest in the constellation Ursa Minor, if you know what I'm saying."

"I've never heard of such a thing!" said Mrs Wood.

"It's obvious, man!" said Euston. "It's the whole reason he's come down here today innit? He's a koala corrupter. A teddy toucher. A Yogi yanker. A Biffo bandit. He's an out-and-out pandaphile…"

"That's enough, young Euston," said Mr Wood firmly. "I can assure you I am no sort of bear pervert!"

"Shouldn't that be a bear-vert?" asked Euston.

"Yes. No. Er… Whatever it is I am definitely not one!" spluttered Mr Wood.

Let's hope he's telling the truth, readers. Telling lies is a very wicked thing.

The actual reason why Mr and Mrs Wood had come to the station that day was to meet their daughter, Rebecca. Rebecca was returning after a few months away at boarding school.

Well, it was a sort of boarding school. It was an establishment with an educational remit situated deep in the countryside which provided residential facilities for its school age attendees.

Okay! It was a youth detention centre in the Midlands. But to Mr and Mrs Wood it was a boarding school. And one with a surprisingly affordable fee structure. Rebecca had been sent there six months ago following an unfortunate incident involving her domestic science teacher and an industrial bacon slicer.

Now Rebecca was being allowed to return home for the hols or, as her school described it, time off for relatively good behaviour on condition that she refrained from operating any item of meat processing equipment within one hundred yards of Mrs (formerly Mr) Thompson.

"Look, there she is! There's Rebecca!" squealed Mrs Wood.

Mr Wood and Euston peered through the crowd.

"Cor! Just look at the jugs on that girl coming towards us," said Euston.

"Do you mind?" snapped Mr Wood. "That's my seventeen-year-old daughter."

"Sorry, squire," said Euston before correcting himself. "Cor! Just look at the jugs on your seventeen-year-old daughter coming towards us."

Mr Wood's face suggested that he found the small, potty-mouthed bear's comments highly irregular. This notwithstanding, Euston continued to extoll Mr Wood's daughter's physical assets in an extremely loud voice.

"Well, they certainly clear a way through the crowd for her! Cor! Just look at the airbags on that! What a plateful of love muffins! What a cartful of magnificent milk melons! I bet she has to walk downstairs fast! I'd love to see her ridin' a bike towards me down a cobbled street. Has she got two small bald men walking directly in front of her? Cor! There's no danger of her falling on her face is there? If she fell over she'd bounce right back up again!"

And those are just the edited highlights of what he said. The little bear had really warmed to his theme.

"Coo-ee, darling!" Mrs Wood waved frantically at her daughter. "Here we are! Coo-ee! Coo-ee! Rebecca, darling! Coo-ee!"

"Hey, missus!" Euston tapped Mrs Wood on an area it was not polite to place your paw. "Could you stop saying 'coo-ee' now please?"

Euston brushed away the twenty or so straggly, one legged pigeons that had descended on him in response to Mrs Wood's coo-ing and which were now pecking at the bits of discarded takeaways embedded in his "Angora jumper."

"Mummy! Daddy! Sowwy I'm late. The twain was delayed at Wugby!" said Rebecca.

"What language is she talking in?" asked Euston.

"Hello, darling," Mrs Wood beamed at her daughter. "How was youth detention centre… I mean boarding school?"

"Oh, it was gweat," weplied Webecca. "It was weally weally twemendous."

Rebecca was not only potentially dangerous but she also had a very irritating speech impediment. Not only that but she was incredibly stupid and had therefore completely fallen for the being-sent-away-to-boarding-school line.

"According to the headmistwess," she continued, "I'm doing weally well at weading, witing, awithmetic, astwonomy, twigonometwy and elocution."

"Has she made you a prefect?" asked Mr Wood.

Rebecca explained they didn't have pwefects at her school but next term she was in line to be one of the older girls' bitches.

"Hello, little girl," said Euston sidling up beside her. "So how would you like a nice teddy bear to cuddle up with in bed tonight?"

"Who is this howwible cweecha?" asked Rebecca. "And why does he have wubber johnnies on his shoulders?"

"Come on! Let's see you try on a little teddy," said Euston winking in a manner that made even Anne Robinson look cute by comparison. "Go on, darling! I'm quite a rare sort of bear so if nothing else just consider the conservation value!"

The little bear then made a crude gesture with his paws to suggest the way in which Rebecca could help him conserve his species.

"Ugh! Mummy, make this smelly thing go away!" squeaked Rebecca.

"Don't be like that, dearie," said Euston. "I'm a wild animal between the sheets… Well, I'm literally a wild animal to be honest."

"Who is this wepulsive wascal?" demanded Rebecca.

"Yes," said Mrs Wood, reaching into her Marks & Spencers carrier bag – they'd been shopping on the way to the station – to produce a baseball cap and a vest. "That's a good point. Who are you exactly?"

Before the little bear could answer, Mrs Wood had used the baseball cap to swipe the offending items from his shoulders before plunging the vest down over his head with the unmistakable dexterity of a woman who has dressed a toddler in a tantrum. She plonked the baseball cap on his head. At least now he wasn't naked, although in the blink of an eye the filth that encrusted Euston quickly infected the vest, making it look like he had been wearing it for years.

Slightly taken aback by the speed of this onslaught, Euston gave a little snarl then explained that he had come from South America.

"Are you from darkest Pewu?" asked Rebecca.

"Darkest where?" sneered Euston. "Did she just ask if I am from darkest pooh?"

No, Euston explained, he had come from even darker Colombia. Even though he was a very small bear he had made the journey from "even darker Colombia" all on his own. This had been difficult especially in the early part of the journey because it is so dark in "even darker Colombia" it is virtually impossible to see anything at all. He had then made the long crossing to England in cramped, dingy, uncomfortable conditions without anything whatsoever to eat.

"Oh dear!" said Rebecca. "Did you twavel as a stowaway?"

"Certainly not," sniffed Euston. "I came over in a first class seat on the Cheapy Jet flight from Bogota."

"I don't believe you didn't have anything to eat on the way," said Mrs Wood dabbing at Euston's face with a moistened hanky. "What's all this orange sticky stuff round your mouth?"

"Yes. Sorry about that, missus. I've been suffering from a very unpleasant cold sore," explained Euston.

Mrs Wood made a mental note to boil her hanky when she got home.

"But why did you come here all the way from darkest Colombia?" asked Mr Wood. "Did your auntie send you?"

"My auntie? No. It was more a sort of godfather really," said Euston. "Come on! Think about it! What do you think is the usual reason for small cuddly furry things to be brought into this country from Colombia?"

"I don't know, I'm sure," said Mr Wood. "Were you a free gift with a jar of coffee?"

"No," said Euston. "I'm more in the Colombian import/ export business."

Euston tapped his nose. The Woods still didn't seem to understand, so Euston tapped his nose again while making a loud snorting noise. Euston then tried telling them that every day was Red Nose Day where he came from. The Woods still failed to get it. They were exceptionally stupid people.

"All I'm saying," explained Euston, "is when I came through customs I was stuffed so full I was about five times

my normal size… and worth several hundred thousand times my normal value."

Euston winced at the memory of being repeatedly stuffed, unstuffed and having his intimate bodily areas sewn back up again by a series of swarthy looking South American gentlemen who were noticeably unskilled in the area of needlework.

Now Euston was attempting to raise money for the journey back home to Colombia. This had been the reason for his hapless attempt to mug every man, woman, child, tramp, dog and one legged pigeon at Euston station that morning.

"Is the ticket to South Amewica vewwy expensive?" asked Rebecca.

"No," said Euston. "It's only three quid on the Cheapy Jet to Bogota. So that's no problem whatsoever. Now all I have to find is the two hundred and sixty five quid I need for the train ticket to get me to the airport."

"Never you mind that, little bear!" announced Mr Wood grandly. "I told you before! You are going to come home with us!"

"You cannot be sewious, father!" said Rebecca, looking howwified.

"He's going to live in our house with us," Mr Wood stated firmly.

Considering that this might be his sole source of income that morning, Euston reminded Mr Wood of the cost of home visits and that there would be an additional charge for any extra thread or needlework that might be required. Well, Euston thought to himself, he'd already had to be stitched and unstitched a few times this week.

"Have you gone stark waving mad?" enquired Rebecca. "Are you off your wocker? Are you weally saying you intend to take this wude, wepulsive, malodowous, putwid, gwime-encwusted cweecha home with us!"

It was a fair description, thought Euston. Nevertheless, it still made him sound like one of the more attractive, hygienic pick ups hanging around the station that day.

"I thought he'd be company for you and your little brother, Jocelyn, who isn't here with us at the moment but who I thought I ought to mention at this point so it doesn't seem weird when he suddenly appears a bit later on in the story," explained Mr Wood.

"He's a ****ing bear, father!" stated Rebecca. "How is a ****ing bear going to be good company for me and my ten-yea-wold, fair-haired, blue-eyed little bwother Jocelyn? What are you going to do next? Hire a man-eating tiger as a babysitter? Bwing home an alligator to pwovide a bit of extwa tuition for GCSE English litewature?"

"Don't be silly, darling," said Mrs Wood.

"I'm not the one who's found a ****ing wild bear wandewing awound the ****ing station and who now wants to take him home and adopt the ****er!" exclaimed Rebecca, now noticeably becoming a little upset. "Whatever you do, Mother, don't take Daddy to the ****ing zoo! He'll come home with his ****ing pockets stuffed. The ****ing house will end up like Noah's ****ing Ark!"

"Now, darling. You know that's not nice language to use," Mrs Wood told her.

"****ing **** you and your ****ing nice ****ing language, you ****ing pair of soppy old ****ers," responded Rebecca.

"Now you know that's simply not physically possible," Mrs Wood told her daughter quite firmly. "Just calm down please, Rebecca darling. You know what I have to do if you start to get too upset."

Mrs Wood reached in her handbag for the tranquiliser gun that a social worker had given her in case of Rebecca having "another one of her turns." If things turned really nasty Mrs Wood wondered if it would be better to fire a dart at her daughter or the wild bear first.

"Now come on, Rebecca! Be reasonable, darling! What else can we do with this poor lost little bear?" demanded her father.

"Yes, Rebecca. Listen to what your ****ing father says," added Euston. "Are you going to let me wander off into the cold inhospitable city or take me home to your warm luxurious mansion?"

Rebecca suggested that the services of the ****ing police, the ****ing dwugs squad, the ****ing vice squad, a ****ing cwack team of ****ing wild animal twappers, the National ****ing Society for the ****ing Pwevention of Cwuelty to ****ing Children and a ****ing taxidermist might all be better options for dealing with Euston.

"I hope you're making a note of all this!" demanded Rebecca of the six-foot-tall man in uniform standing next to her.

"Hang on! Who's this?" asked Euston.

This was PC Rogerson. PC Rory Rogerson was a man who found Rebecca's speech impediment particularly annoying. He was also the policeman who had had been given the job of escorting her back from her "boarding school" and who had been standing alongside her ever since she arrived.

"Strewth!" exclaimed Euston. "I'd presumed your daughter was Siamese twins."

Admittedly, in retrospect, it would have been odd to have

found a pair of Siamese twins with such a clear, twenty-year age difference between them.

Also, Euston considered, the fact that they were merely joined at the handcuffs would have made any operation to separate them much easier than might otherwise have been the case. Not only that, but it would mean the operation could be performed by an ordinary high street locksmith rather than a highly qualified surgeon of international renown.

PC Rogerson consulted his notebook.

"Yes, Miss Rebecca," he said, "so far I've written down details of the following illegal occurrences: 'a wild, dangerous animal at loose in a busy public area. A wild, dangerous animal attempting to intimidate and rob passers by. A wild, dangerous animal who has openly admitted smuggling class A drugs into the United Kingdom.' Now then do any of you happen to know what the name of this wild, dangerous animal is?"

Euston opened his mouth to tell PC Rogerson his full, extremely difficult to spell, South American name when Mr Wood butted in.

"Yes! His name is Euston!" announced Mr Wood.

Euston considered how exceptionally polite the English were. Even if they caught you red-pawed smuggling drugs, even if you had attempted to hold them up at knifepoint you were unlikely to get into trouble because they would take it upon themselves to come up with a false identity to give to the police on your behalf.

"Euston," noted down PC Rogerson. "That's quite a coincidence isn't it? Seeing as we're at Euston station."

"Good heavens! That's incredible isn't it?" said Mr Wood, amazed.

"This man is amazed by the name he just gave me himself," thought Euston to himself, shaking his head sadly.

"Anyway," continued Mr Wood, "you can't charge the poor little fellow. I'm taking him home with me."

PC Rogerson flicked open his notebook again, licked his pencil and then sharpened it with his teeth.

"One further illegal occurrence," wrote down PC Rogerson, "the older gentleman openly admits attempting to illegally re-home the bear without undertaking the necessary quarantine procedures."

"Hey! Never mind that!" said Euston pointing an accusing paw at Mr Wood. "You should be arresting this man for propositioning and attempting to abduct me! He told me he was interested in taking me home to do a bit of bear back riding if you know what I'm saying."

PC Rogerson got his notebook back out yet again and noted, "The bear has also confessed to soliciting for sexual purposes."

"Hey!" yelled Euston. "It's not me you want, PC Plod. It's this lot here. I think you'd better handcuff the whole family together. Go on! Chain them up together so they look like an enormous charm bracelet."

"Awwest this ****ing bear now!" screeched Rebecca.

"Using obscene language likely to offend in a public place," wrote down PC Rogerson on his list of charges.

"Are you ****ing going to ****ing do anything about this or what?" asked Rebecca.

"Calm down now, miss," said PC Rogerson putting his notebook away in his pocket. "I'll submit all the necessary paperwork in the morning. Investigations should commence early in the new year."

"But what about now!" demanded Rebecca. "Aren't you going to awwest this bear? You've got him for loitewing, wobbing, pwostitution and dwug smuggling."

"You missed out entering the country illegally," said Euston.

There was a moment's pause.

"Oops!" said Euston realising no-one had mentioned this particular crime so far.

"So… this bear is an illegal immigrant as well as everything else!" said PC Rogerson. "Well, that puts an entirely different complexion on the matter."

PC Rogerson muttered something Euston couldn't quite make out into his walkie talkie. Suddenly blue lights started flashing and sirens began sounding all over the station. Police cars screeched up outside, helicopters began circling overhead, policemen on horseback assembled by the entrance and a police motorbike display team consisting of eighteen officers balanced on one another's shoulders drove through the middle of the concourse.

"They're quite hot on illegal immigrants these days aren't they?" remarked Euston.

Policemen with shields and batons raced in from all sides. A couple of them spent a few moments attempting to kick in the station's automatic doors but were unsuccessful in this because the automatic doors kept automatically opening. In the end one officer had to hold the doors closed

24

while his colleagues smashed them to pieces. Armed officers took up positions all around the station.

A voice sounded through a megaphone: "OK. Nobody panic. There is no, repeat no, emergency. Will the illegal immigrant here in this station today put his hands up and take a step forward."

Every single one of the thousand people on the concourse put their hands up and took a step forward.

"OK," said the megaphone voice. "All of you put your hands down. Will just the drug smuggling South American illegal immigrant bear put his paws up instead."

Everyone put their hands down apart from Euston and an albino bear dressed in a bright red jumper, yellow trousers and scarf who was standing on the other side of the station.

"What are the chances of that?" remarked Euston.

"Damn!" said Mr Wood. "That other bear is dressed much more cutely than this scruffy tyke."

"There he is!" yelled a policeman.

The squad of armed officers rushed forward and Euston found himself suddenly pinned to the ground with several dozen guns pointing at his head.

"Well, this is ****ing typical isn't it?" remarked Euston his face pressed to the floor.

"What do you mean?" asked the Woods.

"Well," said Euston, "you get a South American on the London underground train system, they have a little run in with the police and look what happens!"

Chapter 2

Whatever The Hell You Do, Don't Let This Bear Into Your House!

Mr Wood waved at the policemen as he drove his car out of the station almost losing control of the vehicle as he did so. This was because he had to wave not just to PC Rogerson but to all the hundreds of other friendly bobbies the Woods had met and been interviewed by that day.

The albino bear in the red jumper and yellow trousers looked resentfully over his shoulder at the Woods' car as it drove past. His bright attire had been his undoing, having caused the police quickly to switch their attention in the assumption that he was some kind of pimp. The other bear was, therefore, now standing with his paws splayed wide against the station wall while having his yellow tartan trousers brusquely frisked by a stocky policeman.

Euston gave him a cheery smile while forming an L for "loser" shape on his furry forehead as they drove by. And that's no mean feat when all you're equipped with is paws.

"My goodness! What an extraordinary coincidence, Mrs Wood!" piped up Mr Wood brightly.

Euston noted that Mr and Mrs Wood did not appear to be on first name terms with each other.

"Did you notice that, Euston?" said Mr Wood indicating the sign over the station entrance. "Your name is Euston and we found you at Euston station! What are the chances of that?"

Euston grimaced. The brain that had just made this comment was the same one that that was in sole control of the vehicle in which he was currently travelling through the dense London traffic.

Euston lifted himself up and peeped out of the car window to see the big city around him. Everywhere bright lights were shining in the darkness and thousands of people were pushing and heaving their way along the pavements. Enormous great buildings towered above him

and magnificent shops lined the roads full of wonderful exciting glittering things.

The little bear looked out wide-eyed and thought to himself, "Give me six months and I will own this ****ing town." And then a moment later he thought: "Hang on. Why is it dark out there? It was morning just a few moments ago!"

"How long have we been sitting in this ****ing twaffic jam?" moaned Rebecca beginning to drum impatiently on the back of her father's seat with a Black and Decker power drill.

Mrs Wood's frantic attempts to sedate and restrain her daughter before she became dangerously agitated helped pass the rest of the journey.

Soon Mr Wood had driven them out of the city centre and into a tree lined avenue of houses. Or, as he very nearly managed to do, out of the city centre and into a tree.

"So, what do you think, Euston?" asked Mr Wood as they drove through a sumptuous looking neighbourhood full of grand looking houses with large immaculately kept gardens. "How would you like to live here?"

Euston thought Mr Wood was asking if he would like to live permanently in the Woods' car and therefore replied that he thought he had spent much of his life to date there already.

They turned the corner from Plantagenet Parkway into Tudor Terrace, Stuart Mews and Civil War Boulevard past the Hanover Lane Gyratory System and then into Saxe-Coburg Avenue before pulling up outside a grand looking house with the number 23 on the door.

"So, little bear! What do you think of this place?" asked Mr Wood. "Ever seen a house that looked as fine as this one?"

"I once saw a brothel that looked a bit similar," remarked Euston.

Mr Wood looked blank. But then that was how he usually looked.

"Would you like to go inside and have a look?" asked Mrs Wood.

"Yeah, I would, and what's more I think we're in luck," said Euston enthusiastically. "The lights are all off. It looks like the suckers who live here are all out."

"Yes and I know the sort of people who live here would love to offer a bit of charity to a small homeless bear," said Mrs Wood.

"Right! I see what you're getting at," said Euston his eyes narrowing. "OK! Keep the engine running!"

Mr and Mrs Wood and their daughter did as Euston had told them. They sat cheerfully in their car while the little bear darted out and through the garden gate. He quickly located a spade from the garden shed and used it to smash his way through the back door.

"Oh my goodness!" said Mrs Wood looking horrified at the sound of shattering glass. "Did you hear that just then?"

There was a continuous sound of loud crashing and smashing from inside the house while the Woods' burglar alarm started wailing loudly and flashing its blue light across their car in the driveway.

"Oh my God!" exclaimed Mrs Wood. "It sounds like we've got burglars and that poor defenceless little bear has just gone into the house all on his own!"

"Oh dear!" said Mr Wood. "Anything could happen to him in there!"

"Euston!" called Mrs Wood out of the window. "Are you all right in there with the burglars?"

Just at that moment the boot of the car was thrown open and the Woods heard the sound of a large quantity of metallic objects of all shapes and sizes being poured in. A moment later a shower of glass items was emptied over them in an ear splitting, shattering cascade. This was followed by the sound of Euston's voice muttering a series of expressions that all seemed to end with the word "hell."

The sound of the car boot being slammed down was followed by more sounds of glass shattering and splintering and yet more expressions which now frequently involved mention of the word "Christ."

A few seconds later Euston hopped back inside the car.

"Right! Drive, you mother!" snarled the little bear.

"But I've never passed my test," insisted Mrs Wood from the passenger seat.

"Step on the gas, mister! Better burn some rubber before the filth gets here or we're all going to be going down for a long time," shouted Euston who was beginning to feel somewhat anxious.

"I'm sorry. You've completely lost me now," sighed Mr Wood shaking his head in happy confusion.

"He said dwive, ****wit!" explained Rebecca helpfully.

"Yes. Take us home, dwiver... I mean, driver," added Euston.

Finally understanding what the little bear was requesting

him to do, Mr Wood turned on the ignition, moved his car two inches further up the drive way and stopped again.

Euston gave Mr Wood a quizzical look which was pointless because Mr Wood was hopeless at quizzes.

"What part of 'take us home' doesn't the stupid **** understand?" squealed Euston.

"But this is where the stupid **** lives!" explained Mrs Wood.

A few moments later the Wood family were stepping into the trashed hallway of their home. The entire house was in a sorry mess. In every room drawers and cabinets were lying thrown across the floors, their contents untidily strewn in all directions.

"Who strew all this?" asked Mr Wood scratching his head in confusion. He didn't remember the house having being in quite this state when they had gone out that morning.

"Oh dear! This is absolutely terrible," sobbed Mrs Wood.

"It is," agreed Euston. "You invite me back to live in your gaff and the place turns out to be an absolute ****hole."

Mr and Mrs Wood hung their heads in shame and told Euston they were very very sorry.

"I should think so too," said Euston.

Rebecca snatched the little bear by his arm.

"Listen, buster, you might be able to twick mummy and daddy into thinking you're all sweetness and light but I know it was you who wecked our wesidence. How did you manage to make such a mess? You were only in here a couple of minutes," she whispered accusingly.

"I can't help it. I'm a quick worker," replied Euston adding with a disgusting wink, "And that might not be the last time you hear me say that this evening, darling!"

Rebecca let go of him and wiped her hand.

"Cor! What a dump!" she exclaimed.

"I know," said Euston looking around at the devastation.

"No. I was refewwing to that dump in the fwont woom," said Rebecca indicating a large, brown mound that had been left gently steaming on the Woods' coffee table.

"Oh yes. Sorry about that," said Euston. "I thought that was something burglars usually did."

It was something burglars usually did but Euston hadn't confined himself to just the coffee table in the living room.

"I don't believe it!" shouted Mr Wood crossly from the kitchen. "I seem to have just trodden in something unpleasant on my marble kitchen floor tiles."

"You cwapped in the kitchen as well!" exclaimed Rebecca.

"Well, it was quite a long journey from South America," Euston explained.

Mr Wood emerged purple faced and brown toed from the kitchen.

"You need to get yourself a cleaner, pal!" said Euston helpfully.

"I've got a housekeeper already," responded Mr Wood. "Her name is Mrs Custard and I really must have a word with the woman."

"You have a housekeeper!" said Euston surprised. "What ****ing century is this again?"

"Well, we don't really like to use the term housekeeper," said Mr Wood. "We prefer to use the term 'servant'. It's less demeaning."

"How," asked Euston, "is being called a servant less demeaning for her?"

"Not for her," explained Mr Wood. "For us."

Rebecca told Euston, "Daddy thinks Mrs Custard is a dear old lady."

"He quite likes her, then," said Euston.

"No," said Rebecca. "He thinks she charges too much for what she does. None of us can stand the fussy old cow!"

The fussy old cow had been in employment at the Wood household for so many years because none of them had been brave enough to sack her.

Mrs Custard cooked, cleaned and looked after the family. Mrs Wood's role in the household, therefore, seemed to be something of an executive consultative position. It seemed that the housekeeper had to do all the jobs that Mrs Wood couldn't be bothered doing herself.

"Oh yes!" said Euston giving Mr Wood a knowing look.

"Not including that," Mr Wood informed him curtly and then muttered, "Not that Mrs Wood is particularly bothered about doing that either."

Just at that moment, Mrs Wood appeared from the dining room and exclaimed, "I can't believe it! Someone appears to have done a number two on my dining room table!"

"You disgusting cweecha," said Rebecca. "How many wooms in this house did you manage to cwap in?"

"Every one of them except the toilet," said Euston, proudly and added by way of explanation, "We have a very high fibre diet in Colombia."

"Did you make all this mess, young bear? I mean – all these messes?" demanded Mr Wood.

Euston was finally beginning to look a bit embarrassed.

"Oh the poor little thing!" said Mrs Wood putting her arm round the small bear. "Don't you see what must have happened, Mr Wood? The burglars must have frightened him so much he couldn't help himself."

These English people were brilliant at coming up with excuses for you, thought Euston.

"Yes! That's right!" he said brightly and then said it

again a bit less brightly while sobbing. "The nasty burglars frightened me. And then they frightened me again. And again and again and again. They frightened me in every single room in the house apart from the toilet which was quite ironic really."

But by this time Mr and Mrs Wood had brought out an industrial sized container of very strong disinfectant and were engaged in the lengthy task of clearing up all the places where the burglars had frightened Euston.

All the while Mr Wood muttered various oaths concerning Mrs Custard, their housekeeper-cum-servant, and the agency that had sent her and how the country had gone to the dogs and how he was going to write a strongly worded letter to the *Daily Mail* about it all.

In the meantime, Rebecca had been given the job of showing Euston around the house. It was a very big, nice house, thought Euston, with lots of rooms. It was a pity, though, that the rooms all smelt so strongly of disinfectant.

"This is Mummy and Daddy's bedroom," she said.

Rebecca showed Euston a large, neat room. Euston had never seen such a big bedroom before. He noted that the size of the room had really helped Mr and Mrs Wood get their twin single beds as far apart from each other as possible.

Next Rebecca showed him a bedroom decorated in pink and adorned with makeup, jewellery, cuddly toys, hundreds of pairs of brightly coloured high heeled shoes and a large poster of Judy Garland in *The Wizard of Oz* over the bed. This was, Rebecca explained, her little brother Jocelyn's bedroom.

Next, Rebecca showed Euston up to a tiny, draughty attic. This was the servants' quarters where Mrs Custard slept or, as her father put it, where the family put Mrs Custard when they weren't using her. There were a great many rooms in the Woods' sumptuous home. Mr Wood had found some difficulty in identifying the smallest available room in which to put the housekeeper.

"What's through that door?" asked Euston indicating a door as Rebecca led him downstairs from the attic.

"None of the west of us are ever allowed into that woom," she explained. "Daddy expwessly forbids it. That woom must hold a tewwible secwet. Sometimes at night you can hear a low moaning coming fwom inside."

Euston suggested that Mr Wood might have locked his mad first wife in this lonely attic.

"No. I think it's where he keeps his stash of pornogwaphy actually," said Rebecca pushing the vile little bear into a tiny box room at the bottom of the stairs. "We thought we'd put you in here," she said. "It used to be my bedwoom when I was thwee."

"Oh this is far too small for me," sniffed Euston. "What else have you got?"

This was, Rebecca considered, a rather presumptuous attitude for someone to take when they had spent the night crapping in almost every room in the house.

"Well, this is my woom," Rebecca told him indicating a room with several dents in the wall, some bomb making equipment on the bedside table, a few bullet holes in the window, a statuette of an extremely well-endowed stallion and a framed photograph of Hitler playing with some kittens beside the bed.

"Oh yes! This is more like it," said Euston turning with a

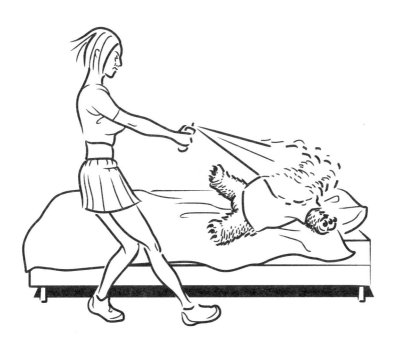

look of lascivious enthusiasm on his face and certain other parts of his anatomy. "So we are alone at last, my darling!"

The small bear then jumped on the bed and started making what he thought was a seductive low gurgling noise. For the next four minutes and twenty eight seconds Euston had an entire can of mace fired with a constant unwavering spray directly into his face.

"Is there something you're trying to tell me?" he asked as he wiped his little eyes while Rebecca shook up a fresh can ready for another blast.

"Get this into your tiny, flea-bitten bwain, you disgusting, foul smelling cweecha," Rebecca told him, "there is no way I am going to share a woom with you."

"Oh," said Euston. "That's a shame. So where are you going to sleep then?"

And before Rebecca could say another word or empty another can of mace, Euston marked the bed as his territory in a particularly noxious manner.

"I like what you've done in here," he told Rebecca admiring the decorative order of the room.

"I'm not so keen on what you've done in here, you fuwwy little ****er!" replied Rebecca dashing to the door before she thwew up.

Later that night when Mr and Mrs Wood were tucked up in their separate single beds and Rebecca was tucked up in the box room in the cot she had outgrown when she was five and Euston was tucked up in his large four poster bed (formerly Rebecca's large four poster bed) in his very own room (formerly Rebecca's very own room) with full en suite facilities (formerly Rebecca's full en suite facilities), the family were woken by a low moaning coming from somewhere downstairs.

"Ohwohwohwo," went the moaning in a low moaning sort of way.

"Oh my goodness! I think those burglars may have come back!" exclaimed Mr Wood as he tiptoed to the top of the stairs.

Mr Wood nervously shone a torch down trying to see if Mrs Wood, who had gone down the stairs five minutes earlier, had found anything.

"Ohwohwohwo," moaned the moaning noise again.

"I think someone's hiding in the under-the-stairs cupboard," said Mrs Wood.

"Wait till I have a word with Mrs Custard about all this!" thundered Mr Wood.

The Woods threw open the cupboard door and there inside they found their young son Jocelyn together with their housekeeper, Mrs Custard. The pair had been blindfolded, gagged and tied up together with gaffa tape.

"Who could have done this?" asked Mrs Wood.

There were some clues to the identity of the perpetrator. There was a smell in the cupboard that suggested Jocelyn and Mrs Custard might have recently been urinated over by person or persons unknown. Even more incriminating was the large steaming brown mound that had been left next to them in the cramped under-the-stairs cupboard.

Mrs Wood removed their blindfolds and the pair blinked up at them in the light.

"Oh yes. There was one thing I forgot to mention," said Euston sidling up behind them. "When we got back home last night, the house wasn't completely empty after all."

Chapter 3

If This Bear Somehow Gets In Your House, Get It Out Again Quick! (Or, Alternatively, Move!)

Rebecca looked at the steaming brown turd that Euston had left in the under-the-stairs cupboard.

"I can't believe the little bastard has **** in every woom in the house," she exclaimed.

"Whose house did you say this was again?" enquired the furry little fellow.

"It's the Woods," replied the Woods.

"Well then!" responded Euston. "I thought everyone knew bears are supposed to **** in the Woods!"

Mr and Mrs Wood and their daughter Rebecca Wood (collectively known as the Woods) looked at one another. They couldn't believe they had been given their name (ie the Woods) solely for the purpose of this one solitary joke. They also couldn't believe it had taken an entire three chapters to get to it.

"Ohwohwohwo," moaned the housekeeper still tied up at their feet.

"My God! What was that noise?" asked Mr Wood who had a very short memory, a very short recall and a very short… oh, er what was it again? Oh, that's it. A very short penis.

"It was that Mrs Custard again," said Euston. "That woman's always moaning isn't she?"

Mrs Custard looked crossly up at Euston. Mr Wood looked crossly down at Mrs Custard. Rebecca looked cwossly acwoss at everyone.

"Oh honestly, Mrs Custard!" exclaimed Mr Wood. "What the dickens do you think you're doing playing round in the under-the-stairs cupboard? Have you seen the state this house is in?"

Mrs Custard's response was muffled and indistinct as a large piece of sticky black gaffa tape still covered her mouth.

"Mmmfffmmmffffmmm," she said.

You see! You can't understand what she's saying can you?

"It's no good, woman! I can't understand a word you're saying," snapped Mr Wood. "What in heaven's name possessed you to tie yourself up and stick that tape all over your hideous, wrinkled, old woman's mouth?"

And with that Mr Wood ripped the gaffa tape off from the hideous, wrinkled, old woman's mouth. This produced a sound not unlike two strips of Velcro being yanked apart. Mrs Custard grimaced. She had just had a fine growth of moustache torn from her upper lip.

She should be grateful for that, thought Euston, examining the discarded strip of gaffa tape. A complete grey moustache looked back up at him. Yes, he thought, that little operation would have cost her a small fortune at a high street beautician's.

Mr Wood set Mrs Custard to clearing up all the mess in

the house for the rest of the night while everyone else went back to bed.

First thing the next morning Mrs Wood heard a muffled moaning sound from the cupboard under the stairs.

"Ohwohwohwo," went the moaning. Well, when it comes to moaning there's very little room for variation. Inside the under-the-stairs cupboard there was also very little room. Not only that but there was also the Woods' son Jocelyn who had been left in there still tied up from the night before.

"I knew we forgot something last night," said Mrs Wood to her husband, as she went to untie him.

Upstairs in his bedroom (formerly Rebecca's) Euston switched on the ornate bedside lamp on the ornate bedside table beside his ornate luxurious king size four poster bed (all formerly Rebecca's) and looked around at the room's facilities (also formerly Rebecca's).

You could see, he thought, that this bedroom's fittings showed real refinement. In fact they showed such refinement it didn't look as though a single one of them had come flat packed. The room had an en suite shower, hot tub, bidet and a gold plated toilet with auto massage facility in the seat.

He picked up the figurine of a well endowed stallion that stood – in more ways than one – next to his (formerly Rebecca's) bed. Euston weighed the statuette in his paws. It was an exquisite and beautifully crafted piece. Euston imagined he would get a good price for it on Ebay. The Woods' house was certainly a place of taste, refinement and intricately crafted stallion parts.

Euston lay back and considered his good fortune.

Yes, he thought to himself, the people who lived in this house were clearly absolute suckers.

It was a very fortunate thing for him that he had been taken in by them and they had been taken in by him (albeit in different senses of the expression "taken in"). In fact, Euston thought to himself, the Woods were such nice people that he had more or less decided to forget the idea of mugging them at all. Instead he had decided to stay in their house and enjoy the benefits of their hospitality for as long as possible.

Well, that would be a little bit like mugging them

wouldn't it? It would just stretch over a much longer period of time.

Euston decided he had now done enough consideration of his good fortune for one morning. Now it was time to get back to his normal attitude. And Euston's normal attitude was one of constant frustration, displeasure and extreme violent anger with everyone and everything he came in contact with.

"Where's my bloody breakfast?" he thought crossly.

He reached over, snatched the exquisite horse figurine and started hammering violently on the floorboards with it.

While he battered the beautiful ceramic horse into a million tiny pieces, Euston yelled and wailed at the top of his voice. Mr and Mrs Wood came running up the stairs to see what was the matter.

"Ah! Mr and Mrs Wood!" said Euston to the panting couple before asking them politely. "Could you fetch the servant for me, please?"

Downstairs, Mrs Custard was just finishing her night's work cleaning and tidying the house from top to bottom. The house had been in such a terrible mess, she thought to herself, it looked as though it had been blown to bits by a doodlebug.

This happy nostalgic image cheered the old lady up no end. How much better things had been in the good old days. Back then the worst that could happen was to have a large incendiary bomb drop through the roof on top of you for the third time that week. Yes, everyone may have been starving, cold, miserable and constantly facing imminent death back then but at least they were happy.

Mrs Custard was cheerfully muttering "make do and mend" to herself as she stuck the two hundred and twenty eight thousand five hundred and sixteen separate splinters of Mrs Wood's shattered crystal glass collection back together with super glue. As soon as she'd finished this she could at last collapse exhausted into her small, uncomfortable bed.

Just at that moment, Mr Wood popped his head round the corner to inform her that her services were required by Euston, or as he now wished Mrs Custard to refer to him, the young master.

"Yes," muttered Mrs Custard, arriving at Euston's bedroom door.

"I believe 'You rang m'lord' was the expression you wanted, Mrs Custard," the little bear corrected her. "Now treat me well, old crone, and you should find me a fair master," he added somewhat imperiously.

Mrs Custard was then set to bathing, dressing and preparing a hearty breakfast in bed for the young master.

Mrs Custard was of the old school. In fact she was of a very old school. It had been closed down before the war. Mrs Custard therefore hardly complained at all as she was forced to do Euston's every bidding. This was despite the fact that it had been "young master Euston" who had made all the mess she had spent the entire night clearing up, it had been "young master Euston" who had tied her up, it had been "young master Euston" who had shut her in a dark cupboard and it had been "young master Euston" who had then climbed on a small stool so he could urinate over her through a keyhole in the cupboard door.

And then while using a warmed, moistened cotton bud

to gently remove the fluff from the young master's navel, Mrs Custard thought again.

"What the bloomin' heck am I doing all this for, for only £3.50 an hour?" she asked herself.

Three pounds fifty would, of course, have represented a full year's wages when Mrs Custard was a young girl, but even so…!

And so the elderly housekeeper proceeded to give a piece of her mind to the young master or as she now took to calling him "the malodorous, villainous, little bear bastard interloper."

Two minutes and thirty seven seconds later Euston and Mrs Custard were standing in front of Mr Wood in his study while Mr Wood docked the old lady's wages. Why Mr Wood should have had a study was unclear as he had clearly never studied anything in his life.

"Mrs Custard, I am very disappointed with the attitude you have shown towards our young guest," said Mr Wood solemnly, "so with immediate effect I am docking your wages to £3.75 per hour."

Mrs Wood whispered to her husband that this would in fact represent an increase in Mrs Custard's wages.

Mr Wood re-checked his calculator. Then, following a series of promptings of "Lower! Lower!" that Euston made from the corner of his mouth, Mr Wood eventually settled on a figure of one guinea per week. All those assembled then expressed themselves happy with this outcome (with one notable exception).

"Cheer up, Mrs Custard!" said Euston cheerfully to the disgruntled housekeeper as they walked out of the door.

"One guinea per week! That makes it a bit more like the old days doesn't it!"

The housekeeper did not look greatly cheered by her new, nostalgia-themed pay packet, particularly when Euston instructed her to "Get a move on, Mrs C! I believe you were only halfway through removing the dirt from my bellybutton this morning and I do suffer terribly from accumulated fluff and foul-smelling, waxy build up!"

"That bear is such a polite little fellow isn't he?" remarked Mr Wood as he watched Euston whipping the housekeeper's backside to get her back to work as quickly as possible.

"Yes," said Mrs Wood, "did you notice he said 'please' and 'thank you' every single time he asked you to lower Mrs Custard's wages a bit further?"

"My greatest regret in life," mused Mr Wood, "may be that our own children seem unable to behave in such as polite and well behaved manner."

"But, Father, what the wuddy heck are you talking about?" asked Rebecca valiantly attempting to control her language, even though she was barely able to believe her ****ing ears. "Last night that bear completely wecked our house and cwapped… I beg your pardon… excweted all over the fwigging place!"

"Now, Rebecca, it's very wicked of you to say such mean and vindictive things about Euston," Mrs Wood told her.

"Yes, Rebecca," said Mr Wood solemnly. "Your mother and I are very disappointed with the attitude you have shown towards our young guest. Step into my study for a moment, would you please."

One minute and twenty eight seconds later Rebecca's

pocket money had been docked to eight pounds and seventeen pence a week.

"Lower! Lower!" called a muffled voice through the ceiling from the bedroom above that had formerly been Rebecca's.

Rebecca's pocket money was indeed docked "lower" and "lower" particularly as a result of all the ****ing language that kept emanating from her every time the amount was docked "lower" and "lower".

Rebecca loudly informed her father that he was ****ing stupid, ****ing ugly, ****ing bald and he ****ing smelt.

Not only that but his ****ing gweat haiwy nose looked from certain angles like a man's ******s.

As she informed her father of these various points, Rebecca emphasised each syllable by drilling a series of holes in his study wall with her Black and Decker power tool.

"This is just the sort of thing I'm talking about," Mr Wood told her. "You'd never ever hear young Euston using that kind of language."

"Watch where you're going with that ****ing cotton bud you ****ing stupid old ****!" growled a gruff bear-like voice from the bedroom above (formerly Rebecca's).

Mr Wood banged on the ceiling in response.

"Enough of that language up there, Mrs Custard!" called Mr Wood.

"Anyway, I know the weal weason you want a bear in this house!" Rebecca snarled accusingly.

"I've no idea what you're talking about," responded Mr Wood, his cheeks reddening slightly as they shifted uncomfortably on the seat beneath him.

"It's ****ing obvious isn't it?" Rebecca told him.

Then, despite the fact it was so ****ing obvious, she went on to explain in a bit more detail.

"It's ever since that wet family in the next woad got one! Ever since they got that stupid little bear of theirs, you've been obsessed with getting one as well!"

"I don't know anything about any other family in this neighbourhood who live with a small, polite bear," replied Mr Wood, clearly lying pathetically and in so doing condemning himself for all time to the eternal fires of hell.

Don't ever lie, readers. It's very wicked.

"It's absolutely ****ing widiculous," said Rebecca. "They dwess the little thing up in a duffle coat and stupid hat and evewything."

"Do they indeed?" mused Mr Wood. "Yes, that is absolutely widiculous."

Despite his claims to the contrary, Mr Wood might have noticed that there was a family who lived in the next road and who had a small bear.

Mr Wood might even have glanced across at their house once or twice and seen the family in the distance having a fine old time with their oh-so-polite, furry, little friend.

Yes, Mr Wood was dimly aware that the family in the next road had their own small bear.

OK, let's not beat about the bush here.

Mr Wood had in fact constructed a small observation turret in the roof of his house which he had then strictly forbidden the rest of his family ever to enter under any circumstances.

Well, as suburban rooftop observation turrets went, it was nothing fancy. It was just a little place where Mr Wood could store his collection of telescopes, night vision binoculars, video cameras, infra red imaging equipment, log books and various bulging albums of long range photographs of the family in the next road and their small bear.

This turret was trained precisely in the direction of the house in the next road. If questioned, Mr Wood would express surprise at where the builders had chosen to position it. Nevertheless it must have been a happy coincidence because once it was built Mr Wood was in there day and night.

But there's nothing wrong with maintaining a healthy interest in what your neighbours are doing is there? As Mr Wood always explained, he merely wanted to make sure that nothing untoward ever happened to the families, whether they had a small bear staying with them or not, who lived in their neighbourhood.

It was, therefore, slightly unfortunate that the observation turret was sited where it was. If, for example, it had been set on the other side of the house, Mr Wood might have spotted that the ninety-year-old lady who lived opposite hadn't taken her milk in for the past three weeks.

Anyway it wasn't just Mr Wood who had become obsessed with that wet family in the next road and their small, polite, well dressed bear. Ever since they'd brought home that irritatingly nice little creature, having a wild animal round your house (preferably one wearing a hat, coat and some form of rubber footwear) had become all the rage in this particular leafy London suburb.

One family had brought home a panda sporting a cagoule, a trilby and a pair of flip flops. Another couple had acquired a hyena wearing a parka, a turban on his head and two pairs of rubber sandals (to cover his four feet). And then there was the family who had appeared one day with an alligator dressed in a puffer jacket, a leather flying helmet and wading boots. Strangely enough, this particular family never appeared anywhere else again after this.

All of these various residents also claimed to have picked their various creatures up at different railway stations in the city.

The giraffe in the skull cap, cycle cape and flippers had supposedly been found wandering around aimlessly at Waterloo. Similarly, everyone had been told that the koala in the burkha, pac-a-mac and fetish boots had been picked up on the escalators at Charing Cross.

Nevertheless, many suspected that their neighbours were acquiring their strangely-dressed furry friends from somewhere off the internet. Indeed, it wasn't long before specialist sites such as reallivebears4u.com and smallwildanimals2go.co.uk began to appear.

These offered potentially savage wild creatures in outdoor casual wear delivered to your door or, if you preferred, left for collection at the London railway station of your choice.

It was for this reason that in recent months the mortality rate among commuters, parcel delivery drivers and middle class families in the neighbourhood had reached worryingly high levels. Other parts of the city might be suffering from the threat of knife and gun crime. In this area, however, residents faced a constant danger that a trip to the local branch of Waitrose might end with them being torn to pieces by a small, savage animal dressed in a panama hat.

The area had become one of the very few outer London suburbs that could boast its very own, full-time game warden.

This was an individual named Klint Van Der Klerk, a swarthy, burly, heavily scarred South African who had been barred from his native land for human rights abuses. This would have been bad enough in normal circumstances but Klint Van Der Klerk had been banned from South Africa for human rights abuses in the early 1970s.

Every day, Klint toured the high street and neatly hedge-lined avenues of the area in his camouflage painted Land Rover. He was a familiar sight in his khaki shirt, shorts, knee length socks and large, brimmed hat as he stalked and prowled the cul de sacs and private roads with his trusty 550 Magnum Safari rifle.

Klint could be regularly seen ducking among the privet hedges and rose bushes or springing out from behind a forsythia ready at a moment's notice to stun, scare or shoot any short, overly hairy figures in hats who appeared likely to endanger the local population.

As a result of this activity, Klint was now the proud possessor of one of the world's most unusual-looking trophy rooms. An entire wall of his office on the high street was bedecked with mounted furry heads, each of which was wearing a jaunty hat or cap.

Also among them was the mounted head of a diminutive, hirsute gentleman. When asked by visitors why he had the embalmed head of a retired merchant seaman on his office wall mounted on a small wooden shield, Klint would inform them that the said Davy O'Donnell had been in the wrong place at the wrong time and it had all been a case of mistaken identity.

Despite the danger of horrific maiming and death that now existed to his family, Mr Wood nevertheless began to salivate slightly at the thought that he had now finally joined the local residents' "Exotic Animals In Funny Hats" club.

There was just one problem. He had not so far managed to coax Euston into a suitably funny hat, the baseball cap donated by Mrs Wood at the station having been mislaid at some point during the burglary debacle. The vest had been removed when Mrs Custard gave Euston his bath and had subsequently disintegrated. So Euston did not have a charming hat. Or, indeed, a cuddly coat. Or even a pair of rubber-based footwear.

Mr Wood jotted down a memo to himself on a scrap of paper: "Must get Euston to try on funny and completely inappropriate clothes including brightly coloured galoshes."

And so Mr Wood revealed himself to be the animal abusing pervert that many of us had suspected for some time.

Chapter 4

Watch Out! This Bear Should Only Be Approached By Highly Experienced Professional Bear Handlers Wearing Protective Clothing Made From Solid Steel – Or Failing That, Get Your Housekeeper To Deal With Him!

Just at that moment Mrs Custard appeared in Mr Wood's study.

The housekeeper was a sorry sight covered as she was in bear scratches, bear inflicted bruises, bear-shaped teeth marks and with a quantity of cotton buds (heavily soiled by foul smelling waxy build up from a range of bear's orifices) that had been embedded (by a bear) in her ears, mouth, eyes and… oh, the woman's head is completely covered in the things, take it from me.

"My but he's a frisky one, the young master," gasped the housekeeper as cheerfully as she could manage before taking a deep breath and asking, "Will there be anything else this morning, Sir?"

"Yes, Mrs Custard," Mr Wood informed her, "I do believe there is."

There then followed a brief embarrassing pause.

The pause lasted until Mr Wood reminded himself exactly what it was he wanted his housekeeper to do next by surreptitiously consulting the memo he had jotted down a little while earlier.

"Ah yes!" said Mr Wood, leading his housekeeper to the cloakroom. "I want you to help dress the young master… by force if necessary… in this outfit!"

And at this Mr Wood plucked an armful of the brightest outdoor togs he could find.

For the next three quarters of an hour, the sound of an old lady wrestling upstairs with a bear and a polyester outer garment reverberated around the Woods' house.

It is, of course, exceptionally dangerous to attempt to dress a bear in a brightly coloured anorak, beret and galoshes against its will. Furthermore, "against its will" is invariably the only way in which the task can be performed. Mr Wood was fully aware of the dangers involved and was careful to take all necessary safety precautions to protect himself and his family. This was precisely the reason why he had made his elderly housekeeper do the job for him.

There was another noise from upstairs not unlike an enormous jelly being dropped from its mould from a great height. This was the sound of the Woods' elderly, overweight housekeeper being sent flying against a bedroom wall.

"I think Mrs Custard and Euston are really beginning to hit it off," remarked Mr Wood brightly.

"Yes," said his wife, "I think sparks will be flying between those two before too long."

Sparks were indeed already flying between Euston

and Mrs Custard but not in the way that Mrs Wood had intended.

It wasn't just bear-related injuries that Mrs Custard was having to endure. The presence of a bright, shiny polyester anorak in the midst of the turbulence resulted in continual crackling and flashing. Repeated small blue explosions lit up the room as a result of the massive build up of static electricity that was being generated by the tussle.

Every few moments Euston or Mrs Custard would emit a pained yelp at yet another crack or spark. At the same time the scent of singed curly grey hair and bear fur began to rise like a mist over them.

After several minutes of what sounded like a sado-masochists' outing to a cattle prod demonstration, one of the mismatched wrestlers finally emerged triumphant from the smoking haze.

"Ah! Well done, Mrs Custard! Thank you!" said Mr Wood as his smouldering housekeeper crawled away attempting to mop up the trail of blood she left in her wake with a J Cloth.

Euston stood before Mr and Mrs Wood and Rebecca. There was very little else he could do.

"Look at the stupid fuwwy bastard! He can't move!" said Rebecca. "Can I set fire to him?"

Mrs Custard had stuffed Euston firmly inside a pair of bright pink galoshes and had squeezed a luminous green beret tightly down over his ears. The housekeeper had then zipped Euston up inside a bright puce anorak so firmly that it was now to all intents and purposes a bright puce straitjacket.

And so, to his immense frustration, Euston found himself completely unable to move his arms. Euston found this particularly infuriating as what he currently most wanted to do was to tear off his beret, galoshes and puce anorak, rip them into a million tiny pieces and stuff them up the first available orifice he could find on Mrs Custard.

"Someone's going to pay for this…. with their genitals!" fumed the little bear as he attempted to erupt from his tightly zipped, polyester quilted confinement.

Mr Wood gazed at Euston wide eyed and open mouthed. And not only that, his zip was undone as well.

"But it is my dream to have my own small bear dressed in completely inappropriate clothing," he muttered although it was difficult to tell exactly what he was saying because he was dribbling so much.

"That's ironic," piped up the little bear, "because when I get myself out of this water cylinder cover thing, I'm going to be your ****ing nightmare, pal!"

"But this is so exciting for my husband to see," Mrs Wood told him.

"He'd better enjoy it while he can then!" announced Euston. "Because by the time I've finished with him I guarantee he'll never be able to experience excitement again."

"Euston doesn't seem to be a vewwy happy bunny," observed Rebecca.

"Yes," said Euston, "and there's three basic reasons for that isn't there? Firstly I'm not ****ing happy. Secondly I'm not a ****ing bunny! And thirdly, you've rolled me up in this pink puffer jacket so not only do I look like I'm going on a camping holiday with Boy ****ing George, I look like I'm his ****ing sleeping bag! Now hurry up and get me out of this acrylic sausage roll!"

"Will there be anything else before I pass out in a pool of my own blood?" gasped Mrs Custard from the corner of the room to which she had slithered.

Mr and Mrs Wood were not completely heartless people. And so, after the aged housekeeper had made them a nice pot of tea, they asked her to phone for emergency medical assistance for herself.

Mr Wood ended up dialling the number himself when he noticed what a mess the old lady was making of the phone as a result of her apparent inability to control her spurting blood.

A few minutes later the doorbell rang.

"That will be the ambulance crew for you, Mrs Custard," Mrs Wood informed her.

"Very good, m'lady," said the ancient housekeeper crawling painfully across the hallway to answer the door to the paramedics who had come to treat her.

Well, strictly speaking, Mr Wood should have called an ambulance for his housekeeper. Mr Wood had, however, been somewhat intoxicated by the thought of dressing up his own furry little bear in a silly outfit. And so, rather than phoning for medical assistance, Mr Wood had accidentally dialled the number of their vacuum cleaner service engineer.

Mr Alf Perkins had thus been summoned to treat Mrs Custard's horrendous wounds. This was a ridiculous mistake for Mr Wood to have made. The call out charge for an ambulance would have been much lower.

"Cor blimey, luv," said the repair man who spoke cockney cliché like a native, "she looks like she's been in the wars!"

"What are you implying, Mr Perkins?" demanded Mr Wood. "Our housekeeper has merely suffered a slight accident while attempting to clean the teaspoons in too vigorous a manner."

"But lord luv a duck, guvnor," said Mr Perkins, "it looks like the old dear's gone ten rounds with a wild animal."

"What a ridiculous idea!" Mr Wood scoffed (he was eating a sandwich at the time).

"I'm telling you, guvnor," insisted Mr Perkins, "this old lady looks like she's been attempting to stuff a small cushion with an angry bear."

"That's enough!" barked Mr Wood in a sudden panic. "I say! Is it just me or is it getting a bit chilly in here? Mrs Custard, I think you'd better take the draught excluder and put it somewhere else!"

"The draught excluder?" croaked Mrs Custard.

"Yes, Mrs Custard," said Mr Wood. "That puce, acrylic, angry looking draught excluder over there. The one with the bear's face sticking out of one end! I think you better take it out of this room!"

Mr Wood was thinking on his feet. They were the most intelligent part of him. He did not want anyone thinking he had been mistreating his little bear. They might then take Euston away from him. And he definitely didn't want anyone doing that. At least not until he had had his fill of dressing Euston in unusual outfits and showing him off to the neighbours.

And so he ordered Mrs Custard to "Take the bear-faced draught excluder and place him... I mean it... somewhere no-one will find it such as the under-the-stairs cupboard."

Obviously, that was where the draught was coming from. Mrs Custard dragged the seething, wriggling draught excluder in the general direction of away.

When she returned, the vacuum cleaner repair man continued binding her wounds with insulating tape. He then used an industrial-sized vacuum to hoover away the dust, detritus and the large number of soiled cotton buds embedded in her hair, nostrils and nostril hair before fitting her with a new bag and filter.

After the housekeeper repair man had gone, Mr Wood ran to the under-the-stairs cupboard. To his enormous disappointment the cupboard was bare of bears.

There was, however, someone else still lying trussed up in the corner.

"Mummy said she was going to untie me and let me out earlier on," explained Jocelyn, "but then it was time for *Bargain Hunt* on the television. She told me she'd come back when it was finished but I think it must have slipped her mind."

"I was expecting to find a small bear wearing an anorak in this cupboard," explained Mr Wood as calmly as he could manage. "You, Jocelyn, are therefore an immense disappointment to me. And not for the first time in your life."

"I'm sorry about that, Father," said Jocelyn "So are you

going to untie me and let me out now?"

But by this time Jocelyn's small voice had been drowned out by the slamming of the cupboard door and Mr Wood's retreating footsteps. Mr Wood thundered up and down the stairs searching for Euston or, as he now kept referring to him, "the furry little light of my life."

In the end, it seemed there was only one room left where the housekeeper could have hidden him.

"Please tell me you didn't hide Euston up there in my secret room!" whispered Mr Wood indicating with a trembling hand the stairs leading up to the attic.

"I thought it would be the best place to hide him," explained Mrs Custard.

Mr Wood's face turned red, his eyes smouldered and wax began to trickle from his ears having melted with the heat.

"Noooo!" exclaimed Mr Wood. "Noooooo!" Mr Wood exclaimed again and then just to make sure everyone was completely clear on the matter "Noooooooooooo!" he exclaimed for a third time with even more "o"s.

Mr Wood had expressly forbidden anyone from going into his attic room or as he called it "father's fortress of solitude in the sky." When the door creaked open the terrible cause of Mr Wood's concern was revealed.

Mr Wood stood breathing in deeply. This could have been taken as a symptom of anxiety except for the fact he didn't seem to breathe out at all. Instead he just stood there continually breathing in, slowly turning bright red while inflating his chest further and further.

In the end Mrs Wood could only conclude that this strange behaviour was an attempt by her husband to expand his chest so much that it would hide the entire wall in front of which he was standing. Mr Wood didn't want anyone, and particularly not Euston, to see what was on that wall.

Luckily, the small, trussed-up bear had been left lying face down on the floor. Mr Wood gave him a gentle kick which sent him rolling towards the door. Rebecca then gave him a hefty boot which sent him bouncing down the stairs. When she turned back, everything suddenly became clear.

"Goodness ****ing gwacious!" she exclaimed.

The attic wall was plastered with several hundred photographs all apparently taken with a powerful zoom lens. The photographs all featured the family in the next road having a lovely time with their small, polite, ridiculously

dressed bear.

"The little bear that father has secwetly taken over one thousand photogwaphs of looks exactly like Euston!" said Rebecca.

"What a coincidence!" exclaimed Mrs Wood.

"No! This is the weason why he wanted a bear of his own!" said Rebecca. "He's been besotted for ages with the bear in the next woad!"

Mr Wood was doing a very bad imitation of looking as innocent as possible.

"Good Lord! What's all this then?" he said in what was meant to be taken as surprise but which, in fact, sounded more like a robot being forced to read the words from a card at gunpoint. "What are all these strange photographs on the wall? And what is that stack of magazines in the corner full of pictures of bears in various unusual poses? Not that I know what's in the magazines because I've never seen them and I've never looked in any of them ever. Although I do know that all the bears featured in those magazines are over three years old - and that's 18 in bear years so it's legal! And anyway I don't believe I've ever been in this room before in my life."

From the bottom of the stairs came the sound of sudden violent tearing. A small acrylic bear explosion had just occurred. Bouncing down the steps had helped Euston rip his way out of the anorak, beret and pair of brightly coloured galoshes in which he had been dressed.

"Hey! That bear's just wuined my best puffer jacket!" screamed Rebecca leaning over the banisters and looking down the stairs.

"Are you all right, my darling... I mean, Euston?" called

Mr Wood.

"Where's that ****ing housekeeper who dressed me up in this ridiculous outfit?" enquired Euston.

For the next few minutes the little bear went on to describe in great ****ing detail all the distressing forms of vengeance he intended to wreak on Mrs ****ing Custard.

"Stop him, darling" Mrs Wood implored her husband. "Euston's gone completely berserk! He's going to kill Mrs Custard!"

"Yes," said Mr Wood. "But looking on the bright side, I don't think he saw any of the photographs."

Chapter 5

Bear-n Baby Bear-n!

Rebecca Wood's favourite person in all the world was her grandfather. He was a sprightly, white-haired, old fellow who, unlike her parents or the British legal system, always had a kind word for her.

Rebecca therefore very rarely hit, stabbed, stole money from, swore at or set fire to her grandfather especially as he had given her the two most precious things she possessed: her Ipod and the exquisite figurine of a prancing stallion that she had kept by her bedside since she was a very small child.

Rebecca's grandfather always liked to keep active and get out in the fresh air. So today he had come round to help the family build an enormous bonfire in the garden so they could burn Mr Wood's extensive and shameful collection of bear pornography.

"Come on, Rebecca! Don't be a lazybones!" called Grandfather.

The apple-cheeked old gentleman was stacking up the bonfire while Rebecca carried out piles of magazines with titles such as *Playbear*, *Readers' Bears*, *Completely Bare Bears*, *Asian Bears* and *The Hair Bear Bunch*.

"Come on, young Euston! Help us build this enormous bonfire up!" called Rebecca's granddad who thought he had made quite a friend of the little bear.

"Remind me again why aren't you dead yet, you stupid old ****er?" responded the little bear, who did not share the opinion that Rebecca's granddad had made a great friend of him.

Euston piled some more material on to the pyre before setting it alight. Rebecca, Euston and granddad stood back and watched as small smouldering paper scraps of bear pornography (many with the name and address of their owner – Mr Wood of 23 Saxe-Coburg Avenue, London – carefully printed on them) went fluttering up over the hedges and into all of the Woods' neighbours' gardens.

It was then that Rebecca noticed some of the other things that Euston had just added to the bonfire. There were a quantity of CDs, magazines, books, photo albums, precious letters from her best friends at her special boarding school, several volumes of diaries and the first draft of a novel entitled "Rebecca Forrest: My True Story." And on top of all these, just beginning to blacken and curl in the flames, was Rebecca's prized picture of Hitler playing with some kittens.

Rebecca stood fuming as indeed did all of her most prized personal possessions.

This was almost as bad as earlier that morning when she had discovered that Euston had been using an electrical item she kept next to her bedside to mix his special South American hot chilli sauce. Rebecca stood uncomfortably wincing at the thought. It was going to take months for that inflammation to go down.

"Oh and by the way," added Euston holding up another of Rebecca's most precious possessions, "your ****ing Ipod's ****ing useless as well!"

Meanwhile across the garden Mr and Mrs Wood were talking.

"So you're saying," asked Mrs Wood of her husband, "the builders constructed that secret observation turret in the roof of our house without consulting you about its design and that you had never once been inside it since they completed the work."

"I swear to you that that's the truth, my darling," nodded Mr Wood as he attempted to carry an extremely large stack of pornographic videos featuring bears past his wife in an inconspicuous wheelbarrow and dump them on the bonfire.

Mrs Wood did not believe her husband would ever lie to her despite the fact that he clearly would. Nevertheless, she had suspected for some time that Mr Wood might have secretly been longing for a small bear of his own. Why else had his first words to the midwife following the birth of their two children been, "Is it a bear?" Why else had his second words to the midwife following the birth of their two children been, "What do you mean it's not a ****ing bear!?"

And then there was all the money he had spent in a vain attempt to get young Jocelyn's entire body transplanted with chestnut brown fur and his ears slightly rounded and moved a bit nearer to the top of his head. Yes, that had been a very dubious cosmetic surgery clinic indeed.

And yet, Mrs Wood thought, her husband's argument for the hugely expensive, painful and completely unnecessary operation performed on their three-year-old son had seemed very convincing at the time.

"Not only do all children love bears," he had told her, "but this will make Jocelyn much easier to spot when he comes out of school as well as saving on us ever having to buy him any clothes."

So could her husband be an insane pervert with a bizarre bear fixation?

With an artificially fur-covered three-year-old and a bear observation turret in the roof, it might have been easy for a suspicious person to put two and two together. Luckily for Mr Wood, his wife was as bad at sums as he was.

Not only that but despite the very best will in the world, despite the natural inclination of any parent to see the best in their offspring and despite the unconditional nature of a mother's love, Mrs Wood wasn't that fussed about either of her children.

She found it difficult to regard either of her offspring as anything less than a bitter and terrible disappointment. She would certainly have returned both of them for a refund if she still had the receipt for them.

Her daughter, Rebecca, was a vicious child. There she was now chasing Euston round the garden screaming, "Give me my MP-thwee back, you ****er. "

Rebecca was a criminal who already had a string of convictions to her name. Admittedly, in retrospect, Mr and Mrs Wood had been asking for trouble when they had their daughter baptised with the name Rebecca Larceny Fraud Arson Blackmail Perjury Wood.

The reason for this unusual choice of names was that Mr and Mrs Wood had accidentally picked up a copy of *A Dictionary of Legal Terms* when they had meant to purchase a *Baby Names Dictionary*.

These were therefore the prettiest names they could find

when they consulted the volume in search of names for their baby daughter and, a few years later, her little brother, Jocelyn Manslaughter Diminished Responsibility Wood.

Rebecca and Jocelyn are of course quite unusual crimes with which to be charged these days but they do still exist in English law.

And so, like many parents these days, Mrs Wood secretly hoped for the day when her daughter would commit a crime so terrible that she would be taken away, locked up and not released back into society until she was old enough to buy her own house.

As for her son, Jocelyn, he seemed very much to be keeping himself to himself these days. In fact, Mrs Wood couldn't think where he'd got to recently.

Inside the house a faint cry of "Mmmmmfff-mmmm," came from the under-the-stairs cupboard.

Yes, if anyone ever asked her why she had allowed a dangerous, foul-mouthed, delinquent wild animal into her family home, Mrs Wood had good reasons a-plenty. Firstly, there was the fact she didn't like her children very much; secondly, her husband had a bizarre fetish about bears and, if that wasn't enough to convince the other members of the Women's Institute that it was a really good idea, there was envy as well!

Mrs Wood was, like her husband, extremely envious of that nice family in the next road who had a bear living with them.

Having a bear in the house really seemed to have brought that family together after various long battles with drink, drugs, teenage pregnancy, drug dealing, drink dealing, teenage pregnancy dealing, arrest, imprisonment, extortion, more drink, more drugs, more teenage pregnancy, gambling addiction, sex addiction, sexual gambling addiction, abduction, abduction by aliens and loss of limbs. Yes, that family in the next road had certainly had one hell of a summer last year.

Hang on!

Or was that a different family?

Yes it was, decided Mrs Wood. All those things had in fact happened to the family who lived in the next road to the family who lived in the next road to the Woods. In other words, they had all happened to her own family, recalled Mrs Wood glumly.

But never mind!

The family who had the bear seemed to be an extremely jolly lot and their bear went beautifully with their interior decor. So, if Mr Wood wanted a bear in the house that was fine by Mrs Wood. After all, what could possibly go wrong?

"Isn't it wonderful though, darling," whispered Mrs Wood gently squeezing her husband's hand, "having a little bear of our own at last just like the family in the next road."

Mr Wood gazed at his own little bear. Euston had escaped from Rebecca's clutches and was now sitting high in a tree.

Down below Rebecca had worked herself into such a state that she was attacking the trunk with her bare teeth. Granddad was imploring her to make friends with Euston while clutching his heart and turning a deep shade of mauve.

Euston sat nonchalantly on his branch using the headphones of Rebecca's Ipod to clean out some intimate

areas he hadn't done earlier because he had run out of cotton buds. At the same time his recent exertions were causing him to constantly regurgitate shreds of the acrylic puffer jacket which he had torn off himself earlier on.

Every few moments a deep phlegmy rumble announced the approach of another well chewed, brightly coloured polyester and saliva pellet which the little bear gobbed with great force and even greater accuracy down at Rebecca's grandfather's head or over the hedge at the Woods' elderly neighbours.

If any of these looked across to see the source of the mushy fibrous globules that had cemented themselves to their foreheads, they would be greeted by the sight of Euston up in his tree vigorously waggling his private bear parts back at them.

On consideration Mr Wood wasn't entirely sure if his little bear was quite the same sort of little bear as the little bear who lived in the next road.

No, if he was completely honest with himself Mr Wood couldn't imagine the little bear that lived in the next road doing many of the things that Euston did.

For a start, he was fairly certain that the little bear who lived in the next road didn't smoke quite as much as Euston. Well, not a crack pipe anyway.

"Oh ****ing hell no! Aaaaaaaaaaaagh!"

Euston had just been giving a passing group of nuns an over enthusiastic waggle of his bear parts when he thought he saw a figure he recognised in the next garden. The little bear had been so surprised, he had immediately fallen out of the tree. Luckily Rebecca's seventy-three-year-old grandfather had broken his fall.

Granddad still attempted to remain good humoured despite the fact that Euston was now sitting right on top of his cheery face.

"Come on, Euston, old chap!" said granddad through a mouth full of furry, farting bear backside. "Why don't you give Rebecca her Ipod back and then you and I can have great fun making a brand new one just for you out of an old cornflakes box."

"And by what miracle of micro-electronics is that going to work? Remind me not to buy anything from this old codger's electrical shop!" remarked Euston to Rebecca. "By the way, I've just deleted all your favourite songs and re-loaded the device with 15,000 sound effects of farting bears. Or did I just produce them all myself in a live, unplugged performance?"

Granddad lay attempting to remove a pubic bear hair from his false teeth while gasping for air and longing for the Mickey Mouse gas mask he had been given in his youth during the war.

Euston re-lit his crack pipe from the bonfire of blazing photographs and pornographic bear magazines and gave the nuns peering through the garden gate another waggle before plopping himself back down on granddad's gasping face.

"You know, darling," said Mrs Wood, "the little bear in these smouldering long range photographs does look remarkably similar to Euston. The pair of them could almost be twins!"

At this Euston's eyes bulged, his chest swelled and so did another part of his anatomy.

"Show me those photographs," he demanded snatching up one of Mr Wood's photographs of the other bear.

The little bear froze to the spot when he saw it. He took a deep breath and immediately began choking. He had just inhaled a crack pipe. Euston peered through the hedge at the bottom of the garden.

No! Surely not!

It couldn't be!

But it was!

Impossible!

It's true!

No!

Yes!

Never!

It is!

Ohhhhhh!

Get used to it, baby!

No way!

Oh ye….. How long is this going to go on for exactly?

The little bear glanced furiously backwards and forwards. First he glanced furiously through the hedge, then he glanced furiously at Mr Wood, then he glanced furiously at Rebecca who was trying to administer artificial resuscitation to her grandfather and then finally and most furiously of all he turned to the photographs that all showed a second little bear who looked just like him. This was the figure he thought he had seen and that had caused him to fall out of the tree.

"So do you know this other little bear, Euston?" asked Mrs Wood.

Euston's eyes narrowed.

"No," he said shortly. "I've never seen that other little bear who looks almost exactly like me before in my life."

He was lying.

Euston stared at the photographs. He couldn't believe what he was looking at. The pictures were all completely out of focus. Mr Wood was utterly useless at everything. And yet somehow he had managed to acquire an attractive wife, two kids, a large luxurious house and a great big car. It's annoying when extremely dim people do incredibly well in life isn't it?

Euston looked through the hedge and scanned the house in the next road.

And then Euston saw the thing he most feared in all the world that didn't involve Mr Wood undoing his trousers.

There was the nice family in the house in the next road having a jolly old time with another small bear. There they were all in the kitchen laughing together with the other little bear causing various amusing misunderstandings while clearly eating the nice family out of ****ing house and ****ing home.

"Oh no!" snarled Euston. "That is the most pathetic thing I've ever seen."

"I'm sorry," said Mr Wood doing his trousers back up again.

"Oh that is completely pathetic!" grumbled Euston. "A poncey middle class family who have adopted their own little bear."

"Yes, that is the most pathetic thing we've ever heard of as well," said Mr and Mrs Wood.

"Mummy!" called Rebecca. "You better help me get gwanddad inside the house. He seems to have stopped bweathing!"

Chapter 6

Bloody Hell! There's Two Of The Bear-stards!

Over the next few days two faces could be seen inside Mr Wood's top secret, clandestine, completely-unknown-to-anyone observation turret that jutted out from the top of Mr Wood's roof plainly for everyone in the neighbourhood to see.

At any time of the day or night the face of a small bear could be seen scowling down through a pair of binoculars aimed directly at the house in the next road.

Next to him sat a middle aged man armed with another pair of binoculars.

The small bear sat looking out of the window through a pair of binoculars observing every movement that occurred in the house in the next road.

At the same time the middle aged man sat with his second best pair of binoculars pointing directly at the small bear sitting right next to him.

Despite having their binoculars pointing in completely different directions, both the small bear and the middle aged man kept saying the same sorts of things to themselves.

"Oh ****ing hell! Look at the furry little bastard!" the small bear would mutter crossly under his breath. "Oh! Just look what he's doing now!"

At the same time the middle aged man would gaze lovingly at the small bear next to him and also regularly mutter, "Oh ****ing hell! Look at the furry little bastard! Just look what he's doing now!" but with a noticeably more lascivious tone.

"So," whispered Mr Wood sidling closer to Euston, "you like looking at bears as well do you?"

Euston scowled at him. "Yes I do," he said, "but at least I have the excuse that I *am* a bear."

Euston snatched up his binoculars again and continued with his round-the-clock spying on the bear in the house in the next road. A casual observer might have thought his low opinion of the other little bear was excessive, perhaps even unwarranted.

"Oh! Just look at him eating that sandwich," Euston said squinting down at the kitchen window of the house in the next road, "just like the ****ing **** he is. Now look at him - going to the front door to collect the milk… just like the ****ing **** he is. Oh now look! He's gone into the living room to watch the television."

"Just like the ****ing **** he is?" suggested Mr Wood.

"Oh, so you find him as annoying as I do then?" enquired Euston brightly.

This in depth, expert commentary and assessment of the other little bear's behaviour went on all day and all night.

Every single thing that the other little bear did only seemed to help confirm Euston's opinion of him.

He got up in the morning like the ****ing **** he was.

He got dressed like the ****ing **** he was.

He got washed and brushed his teeth like the ****ing **** he was.

He went to the toilet like the ****ing **** he was.

He went down for breakfast like the ****ing **** he was.

And so he continued through the day in a manner entirely consistent with being the ****ing **** he was.

It wasn't long before Mr Wood began to wonder if Euston was under the impression that the other little bear was a ****ing ****.

Euston squinted into the darkness through a pair of night vision goggles. The other little bear was in his room tucked up in bed.

"Look at him lying in his bed fast asleep not moving or doing anything whatsoever like the ****ing **** he is," muttered Euston. "But I can tell he's thinking of something nasty," he added defensively. "Yeah, he's clearly dreaming of doing something really horrible to a small, defenceless puppy."

Euston decided that it was time to take a short break from his round-the-clock observation. So he went outside to relax by doing something really horrible to a small, defenceless puppy.

Even that didn't cheer him up for long. He hated that other little bear. And what's more that other little bear wasn't just *any* other little bear. That other little bear was the same other little bear that Euston had feared he was. He was the same bear that had haunted Euston all his life. His sworn bitterest enemy. Oh, yes. Euston knew him all too well.

What was his name again?

He ought to be able to remember. After all, the little bastard was none other than Euston's own identical twin brother.

Oh, yes! That was it!

Euston remembered that his twin brother's name was Quezalotocacaquezl The Abundantly Fertile One And Bloody Avenger Of The Sun God.

At least that was the name he had gone by in South America. No doubt since illegally entering Britain he would have adopted some different, pathetically soppy name.

It had been embarrassing having a twin brother called Quezalotocacaquezl The Abundantly Fertile One And Bloody Avenger Of The Sun God. It was especially embarrassing when your parents had then decided to give you a slightly less dramatic sounding name, thought Euston (formerly known in South America as Pepe).

All through his cub-hood Euston (aka Pepe)'s mother and father had said to him, "Why can't you be more like your brother? Why can't you be as clever as your brother? Why can't you be as considerate and polite to everyone as your brother? Why can't you be as talented as your brother and as good as he is at everything he turns his little paw to? Why, oh why, oh why, Pepe, can't you be more like your brother Quezalotocacaquezl?"

There were two simple answers to these questions.

The first was, "Because Quezalotocacaquezl is a ****ing ****!"

And the second was, "Because Quezalotocacaquezl's ****ing name is Queza-****ing- loto-****ing-caca-****ing-quezl and mine is ****ing Pepe!"

No doubt Euston's parents would have responded to this by saying, "Oh yes. We hadn't thought of that. Good point, son. Quezalotocacaquezl! Come here! Your twin brother has just pointed out to us the unarguable fact that you are in fact a ****ing ****. So there's nothing for it but for you to **** off and leave us forever!"

Unfortunately, that did not happen. This was because just at that precise moment Euston's father, Pepe senior, and his mother, Quezalotocacaquezella, were horrifically squashed to a pulp.

Yes, right in front of his eyes Euston had just seen his parents run over by an enormous timber lorry that had arrived as part of a convoy sent to carry out a massive deforestation programme on their part of the South American jungle.

And that sort of thing can upset a young bear at a delicate stage in his development.

And so Quezalotocacaquezl and Pepe had to go and live for a while with their Auntie who was the godfather of the local drug cartel.

Euston recalled how Quezalotocacaquezl hadn't seemed quite so bothered about the unpleasantly squishy fate of their parents. In fact once or twice Euston recalled overhearing Quezalotocacaquezl and their Auntie discussing a large sum of money that had recently come Quezalotocacaquezl's way as a result of the sale of land rights to an area of virgin forest.

Quezalotocacaquezl intended to use this mysteriously acquired cash to fund his relocation to England and this plan had very much met with the approval of his Auntie (the well known godfather of the local drug cartel).

And now Queza-****ing-loto-****ing-caca-****ing-quezl (or whatever he was calling himself these days) was here living in the next road to Euston.

That was just typical of him. As soon as Euston had set himself up nicely he discovered his twin brother had got himself an even cushier number with an even soppier, stupider family. If such a thing were possible.

But what exactly was Euston's much loathed twin up to?

Were there any areas of virgin rain forest in this part of North London that he was intending to claim and sell on to developers?

No doubt Queza-****ing Goody Two Shoes had taken the family in the next road in and charmed them with his cute little bear act.

Euston had had to put up with it all through his cub-hood and he wasn't going to put up with it any more.

It was time, thought Euston, to wreak his terrible revenge.

Whatever his brother was up to, it was all about to end. And when it ended, Euston decided, it would end in disgrace, it would end in embarrassment, it would end in deportation, it would end in shame.

Euston mused further.

It would end in discomfort, it would end in pain, it would end in misery, it would end in humiliation.

Euston thought about it a bit more.

And, if at all possible, he thought, it would end in a large barrel of rancid horse manure.

Up in the observation turret Mr Wood had taken over observations in Euston's absence. Dutifully he was regularly noting that the other little bear was lying asleep in bed like the ****ing **** he was although at one point he had got up and gone to the toilet like the ****ing **** he was.

Mr Wood carried on making these useful observations for the next eight hours. In the meantime Euston himself went to bed and lay there snoring loudly like the ****ing **** that he was.

The next morning Euston awoke relaxed, refreshed, content and intent on carrying out a terrible and evil revenge on his twin brother.

And so as soon as he jumped out of bed Euston tried

phoning the RSPCA. He informed the lady who answered the telephone that a wild bear was terrorising the neighbourhood.

"He is a particularly dangerous and evil creature," Euston informed the RSPCA lady, "so bring your maximum strength tranquiliser darts. In fact, you better make sure you sharpen the ends so they'll really hurt when they hit his arse. I mean… so you can be sure to knock him out and save the local children from any further savage bear attacks."

Euston added that it would be easy for the RSPCA to recognise the bear because he would be wearing completely ridiculous clothes.

After a couple of minutes there was still no sign of an RSPCA hit squad roaring round the corner with sirens screaming.

Euston therefore decided that he would pop outside and have a word with the bin men instead. Perhaps they would be able to help him dispose of his problem.

Euston found them in the front garden emptying the Woods' wheely bin over the lawn while trying to decide whether or not to report Mr Wood for not doing his recycling properly.

"Er hem, filth encrusted gentlemen!" said Euston before asking if they wouldn't mind throwing the small bear from the next road into the back of their cart. "Just chuck him in the crusher. If anyone asks, just say you mistook him for a furry bin bag."

The bin men looked at one another. If there's one thing bin men can't resist it's a small grubby bear.

Euston spent the rest of that day tied to the front of the dustbin lorry like a little mascot. The small bear endured an entire tour of every street in the neighbourhood while crucified on the front of the bin lorry which travelled at an average speed of five miles an hour.

As he trundled through the avenues, crescents, groves and mewses of the area Euston cursed the bin men, he cursed anyone else within earshot and he cursed the fact that his backside was constantly smouldering on the sizzling metal of the lorry's radiator grill.

The little bear staggered home later that day, smelling of old takeaways and with the fur on his backside still smoking.

"At least I don't look as bad as he does!" snorted Euston.

"He" referred to Rebecca's ailing grandfather who was lying on the sofa while Rebecca and Mrs Wood tended to him. Granddad hadn't been the same since a wild bear had fallen out of a tree on top of him. Well, you wouldn't be would you? Particularly when the bear had then sat on your face for five minutes while suffering a severe bout of flatulence.

"Yes," said Mrs Wood. "The ambulance is taking a bit of time to get here."

Mrs Wood was beginning to wonder if Mr Wood remembered to phone the emergency services as she had asked him to do three days earlier.

"Anyway, Euston," said Mrs Wood, "at least you don't look like the other little bear any more."

"That's what I've always told you," said Euston. "That

****ing soppy little ****ing **** looks nothing like me!"

"I know," said Rebecca. "He's much better dwessed!"

"Better dressed!" Euston snapped crossly. "I'll show you who's better dressed! Take me to the ridiculous bear outfitting shop this minute!"

Mr Wood's eyes blazed. He had accidentally just set fire to his eyelashes while trying to light his pipe.

And so it was that the Woods set off to the shops to buy Euston a completely ridiculous and highly inappropriate outfit.

Mr Wood's car glided down Saxe-Coburg Avenue. Really he should have driven it down the road but he had hit a speed bump a bit too quickly.

"Oh look! There's Mrs Carmichael the chairman of the local Conservative association, Mr and Mrs Brentwood from the parish council, Mr and Mrs Smythe and their six small children all aged under 11, the local vicar, the Right Reverend Reverend Wright and a group of nuns," said Mrs Wood pointing from the passenger seat at the bus stop ahead of them as the car landed with a thud. "In fact every single one of our most respectable neighbours is waiting in an orderly line for the bus."

"What a fantastic opportunity!" said Mr Wood, rubbing his hands with such glee that he nearly lost control of the car, almost taking out every single one of his neighbours in the process. "Do us a big favour would you, Euston? Could you let all of our neighbours – all of whom are waiting in a long orderly line at the bus stop – know that the Wood family now have their very own small bear?"

The little bear obligingly wound down his window while Mr and Mrs Wood smiled and waved cheerily to their neighbours.

Just at that moment a voice piped up loudly from the back seat.

"Oi wankers! Yes! You ****ing stupid old ****s standing at the bus stop!" Euston called out to them while indicating Mr Wood with an obscene paw gesture. "This ****'s only gone and got himself a ****ing bear hasn't he?"

And then just as Mr Wood's car passed the bus stop Euston poked his furry brown little bear buttocks out of the windows at the Woods' open mouthed neighbours.

"Well," said Rebecca, "they all know we have our own bear now."

Bog Standard was the name on the front of the local outdoor wear superstore specialising in Wellington boots, waterproof clothing and other items needed for wading around the local bogs in that part of north London.

The manager of the shop knew all about the local residents bringing in their alligators, tigers, lions and other highly dangerous wild animal friends to be kitted out in completely inappropriate anoraks and wading boots. He had read about it in the previous manager's obituary notice in the local paper. Not only that but the shop now boasted its own specialist fitting room complete with chains, dart guns and wild animal handlers.

"And what sort of outfit is the young bear interested in?" intoned the manager of the store.

"The young bear wants the sort of outfit that will make him look a complete and total pillock!" exclaimed the young bear. "Or at least as much of a complete and total pillock as this ****!"

And with this, Euston waved a singed, long range photograph of his twin brother at the outdoor wear shop manager's face. The shop manager was predictably entranced.

"Oh yes. I recognise that young bear! He's a lovely fellow isn't he?" said the manager examining the picture.

"He's so well mannered and yet so engagingly clumsy and mischievous."

"Or to put it another way," said Euston putting it another way, "he's a ****ing ****!"

"I'm afraid you'll never get your bear to be like this bear in the picture," the shop manager told Mr Wood.

"How dare you!" said Mr Wood.

"I'm afraid this bear of yours has no breeding," sniffed the shop assistant.

"I think you'll find he has quite a lot of bweeding actually," said Rebecca. "In fact he keeps showing me pictures he's taken of himself bweeding."

"No. I meant he is a very common sort of bear," retorted the shop assistant.

"You'll take that back this instant!" barked Mr Wood. "He looks exactly like the other bear."

"They may look identical but the difference between them is all too clear," simpered the oleaginous shop assistant. "This bear in the photograph is clearly a nice, well mannered, middle class sort of bear. Sir's bear isn't. Sir's bear is… how can I put it politely… sir's bear is a chav bear!"

"How dare you call my bear a chav bear, sir!" ejaculated Mr Wood. And that shows you just how excited he was by the situation. "My bear is not a chav bear! That is the most appalling slander I have ever heard in my life!"

"Hey! I've finally found an outfit I like!" said a voice from behind them.

They all turned and beheld Euston emerging from the changing room behind them dressed in a shiny silver shell suit, a Burberry cap, a pair of over-sized trainers and a small van load of chunky jewellery. Euston looked like the love child of Jimmy Savile and a midget wolfman.

"Check it out!" said the small chavvy bear clutching his crotch in one paw like a bad ass rapper and thrusting it at Rebecca who was thowoughly unimpwessed and who immediately aimed a heavy boot at the paw in question.

This sent Euston tumbling out of the shop door and into the high street. And then just as he picked himself up from the pavement, he was hit in the buttock by a large, specially sharpened tranquiliser dart.

"There he is!" said the RSPCA warden looking very pleased with himself. "One small bear dressed in ridiculous clothing! Got him!"

Chapter 7

How To Get Rid Of An Unwanted Bear

Euston leafed through a copy of Yellow Pages. He didn't think it was a very useful book. It didn't seem to contain any entries for any of the sorts of services he required.

There was nothing whatsoever listed for Hit Men or Professional Assassins under "H" for "Hit", "M" for "Men", "P" for "Professional" or "A" for "Assassins". Euston tried looking under "D" for "Death Squads", "H" for "Hired Killers" and "F", "B" and "M" for "Freelance Bear Murderers". Still he couldn't find anything.

This book is useless, thought Euston. The person who wrote it should be shot. Clearly, though, this was a difficult matter to arrange.

Euston's encounter with the RSPCA had not gone happily.

After Euston's call, an inspector had duly been dispatched. He had quickly picked up Euston's twin brother and shoved him in the back of his van. Then, as he was driving back along the high street, he had noticed Euston coming out of the Bog Standard outdoor wear shop. Euston was dressed in even more ridiculous clothing than the bear he had already picked up. Euston's twin brother was therefore immediately released while the inspector shot Euston with a specially sharpened dart

and carted him off to the local RSPCA animal hospital instead.

At the animal hospital a vet prepared to perform an operation that would ensure Euston calmed down, stopped terrorising the neighbourhood and would be unable to produce any offspring likely to do the same.

"Bollocks!" said Euston realising his fate.

"Exactly," said the vet.

Yes, Euston was about to experience a 66.6% reduction in the number of genitals he had available to waggle out of the window at passing nuns. The vet informed him that the operation would help Euston stop feeling so aggressive and angry all the time. Euston disagreed with this argument quite strongly. In fact if there was one thing guaranteed to make him aggressive and angry this was probably it! Nevertheless the vet staff managed to keep the little bear restrained on the operating theatre table.

Not only was this all embarrassing enough but a film crew from an early evening TV show about vets had turned up to record the event for posterity.

This is very undignified, thought Euston.

The vet prepared to place Euston's most sensitive areas beyond all possible use. As he reached for the anaesthetic, the little bear just managed to raise his head far enough to sink his teeth into the softest area he could reach. The vet screamed so loudly that his shocked assistants immediately lost their hold on Euston.

Millions of the TV viewers watched as the vet leapt backwards from the operating table with a small, very angry bear dangling from his crotch. In evident discomfort the vet waddled painfully around the room with his eyes bulging while his wincing assistants attempted unsuccessfully to detach Euston from his private parts with a window pole.

True professional that he was, the vet managed to remember that the whole event was being broadcast live on television and therefore avoided swearing during the ordeal.

"Oh flipping heck!" he said as cheerfully as he could under the circumstances. "Oh dearie me! Oh dearie dear! Oh this does smart so!"

And so ironically one person in the surgery that day was left unable to have children, but it wasn't Euston.

Euston continued thumbing through the Yellow Pages. The nearest he could find to the service he wanted was Rentokil. When he called them however, they informed him that they were not as he had assumed the English version of the mafia.

Instead Euston tried phoning Mr Jones, the manager of "Get Stuffed", the local high street taxidermist. Mr Jones said he would be very happy to stuff a small bear for him. In fact, Mr Jones told Euston, nothing would give him greater pleasure. Unfortunately however Mr Jones was not able to offer the service of killing the bear in question first.

"Well, couldn't you just stuff him anyway?" suggested Euston. "He'd have a job surviving that wouldn't he? Just keep putting more stuffing in the little bugger till he stops moving."

Mr Jones, who was a highly reputable taxidermist, had already put the phone down.

Back downstairs Rebecca and her mother were anxiously waiting for news from the hospital of granddad's condition. Why they were waiting for news was a bit of a mystery because the Woods had found the old boy lying dead on their sofa when they got back from buying Euston his shell suit. It was therefore a matter of purest optimism to expect any significant change in his condition other than gradual decay.

But then suddenly the phone rang. Then it rang again. And then it rang again. And then it…

Will somebody answer that phone for goodness sake!

"Hello!" said Mrs Wood. "Hello?... Hello?... Hello!... Hello, Mrs Custard! Could you come and answer this phone for us please! Where on earth has that woman got to recently?"

Rebecca snatched up the phone and listened with a howwified look on her face. It was the hospital. They had just performed a post mortem on granddad and were phoning with important news. Would the Woods be interested in purchasing a commemorative DVD of the operation complete with introduction by the chief surgeon at a special purchase price? Oh and by the way initial tests suggested the old man died as a result of asphyxiation due to inhalation of methane.

Mrs Wood put an arm round her daughter. It was the only way she could reach her handbag to get her credit card to order a copy of the DVD.

Rebecca ran sobbing up the stairs. It is an upsetting thing to learn that your grandfather has been asphyxiated by a bear's bottom. At least, though, Rebecca had something by which she could always remember her dear old grandfather.

The door to Euston's (formerly Rebecca's) bedroom creaked open and Rebecca tiptoed in to retrieve the beautiful horse statuette that her granddad had given her to cheer her up after the police had taken her bacon slicer away.

The statuette did not seem to be where she had left it on her bedside table. Where on earth has that wepulsive little bear put that delicate statuette, wondered Rebecca as she crunched her way across the floor.

"That's funny," she thought. "My bedwoom didn't use to have such a cwunchy carpet."

In another room Euston was still considering how to get rid of his brother. It looked like there was nothing for it. Euston would have to do the job himself despite the fact that he would probably end up with a criminal conviction.

But then there were lots of other things he might also end up with.

A nice furry scarf. A lovely tea cosy. A furry hot water bottle cover. A big hat for a soldier at Buckingham Palace. One of those furry little carpets you put around the bottom of the toilet. An unexpectedly lush merkin.

Yes, thought Euston, there must be lots of ways in which he could surreptitiously dispose of the remains of his identical twin brother.

No-one would suspect a thing or guess where the little bastard had disappeared to. Not when Elton John appeared on stage be-decked with a brand new furry wig to keep him warm during a winter tour of the former Soviet Union.

Not even when one of the Queen's guards appeared at trooping the colour wearing a hat that appeared to be 50% bearskin and 50% duffle coat complete with little wooden toggles.

He might end up convicted as a fratricidal bear murderer but surely his environmental friendliness in attempting to recycle the remains would be taken into account during sentencing.

In fact, come to think of it, his little bastard twin brother was so popular with everyone it might be worth trying to sell some of the furry products into which Euston was planning to convert him.

They'd go like a bomb on Ebay!

Euston could see the listings already!

A furry hood with a stupid hat already attached to it. A duffle coat with a genuine fur inner. An authentic famous pair of wellies complete with extra special fur lining.

There could be quite an extensive range of exclusive novelty products.

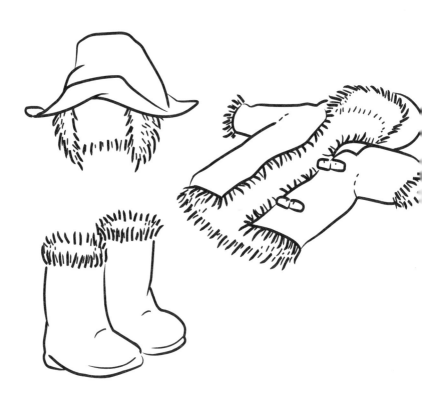

But would there be enough of the little git to go round, wondered Euston. He wasn't a very big bear.

No, Euston would probably only get a rather small rug and half a mitten out of his brother. Wasn't that just typical of the mean little sod?

If that was all the merchandise he managed to produce, Euston probably wouldn't make much more than a tenner before the police tracked him down via his Paypal account.

Maybe, thought Euston, he could get a bit more material off his twin brother if he fattened the little bastard up a bit before he bumped him off.

Or even better, why not bump him off by fattening him up a bit?

This was a brilliant idea, thought Euston.

It shouldn't be too difficult to tempt the greedy tyke with a marmalade sandwich so big, his furry little heart would explode a few seconds after he had finished stuffing himself with it.

Meanwhile, downstairs the Wood family were plotting to get rid of another small bear.

"So you see," explained Mrs Wood to her husband, "Rebecca and I think you might have been wrong about Euston."

"You mean he's not a bear after all," said Mr Wood. "Has he been lying to us? Is he just a very hairy midget?"

"No," said Mrs Wood as patiently as she could, "but we think that it would be best for the family if we got rid of him now."

"That's the most terrible thing I've ever heard," declared Mr Wood. "What has the poor little fellow ever done wrong?"

"He's a psychopath," shrieked Rebecca from the kitchen where she was tooling herself up with knives and any other sharp kitchen utensils she could find.

"Yes," said Mrs Wood, "and not a very polite one at that."

"He may be a psychopath," said Mr Wood, "but he's also a very cute little bear which helps even things out a bit."

"He killed Rebecca's grandfather!" said Mrs Wood.

"Yes, and you two just seem to keep going on and on and on about it," replied her husband.

Rebecca appeared in the doorway brandishing an egg whisk

"He killed my gwandfather!" she woawed at her pawents. "Get wid of the little bastard now or I will be forced to take my tewwible wevenge!"

"So, Mr Wood," said his wife who still hadn't managed to remember her husband's first name. "You have a decision to make before your daughter gets herself into even more trouble. Are you going to side with us – your family – or with him – that wicked little bear?"

Mr Wood weighed this up in his head. It certainly was a no brainer. And so was the decision he was trying to weigh up inside it. There was only one option. He had to side with his family against the evil wild animal he had stupidly brought into their house. It was time to give Euston his marching orders.

Just then a voice called from the top of the stairs.

"Oi! Disgusting pathetic animal abusing bear-vert ponce features!" yelled Euston.

Mr Wood was the only person who, upon hearing this description, turned his head.

"I've got a job for you!" called Euston as Mr Wood eagerly pushed past Rebecca and dashed up the stairs.

The slow, menacing sound of a handheld mechanical egg whisk began to rattle in the still afternoon air.

Upstairs, Euston told Mr Wood that he was now feeling slightly guilty about the attitude he had displayed towards his brother.

"I am now feeling slightly guilty about the attitude I have displayed towards my brother," announced Euston.

See. I told you.

Euston had to admit that his dislike of his twin brother might have begun to seem a little disproportionate. He had to do something to stop himself feeling this way. There was therefore only one thing for it. Euston had decided to set about getting rid of his twin brother once and for all. He was determined that his twin brother should suffer for his terrible crimes.

"Er, what exactly are his terrible crimes?" enquired Mr Wood.

"His crimes against humanity are many and varied," proclaimed Euston struggling to think of any. "Erm... er... Murder. Rape. Never buys a copy of *The Big Issue*. And genocide while wearing a duffle coat."

"That cute little bear in the house in the next road has committed all those terrible things?" asked Mr Wood.

"Oh yes!" said Euston confidently.

"Including genocide while wearing a duffle coat?" enquired Mr Wood.

"Definitely," snapped Euston. "Well… he's got the coat hasn't he? So he's half way there. Similarly he is also 50% guilty of assassinating the Archbishop of Canterbury while wearing a stupid floppy hat and half way to committing arson in a naval dockyard while being a ****ing ****."

And that was why Euston decreed that they had to get rid of the other little bear in the next road. There is only one sentence that can be passed on those found guilty of such terrible crimes. And with these words Euston produced a small black handkerchief and placed it upon the top of his head.

"You're going to sentence him to wear a small, black toupee for the rest of his life?" asked Mr Wood.

"No!" snarled Euston. "It's death isn't it! When a judge puts this little black hanky on his head it means a sentence of death!"

"Why does it mean that? Is it very heavy?" asked Mr Wood.

"No!" said Euston. "I'm just saying there's nothing else for it! The furry little bastard must die!"

And with this Euston laughed an evil laugh which didn't actually sound that evil because he was only a couple of feet tall and had correspondingly short, high-pitched vocal cords.

Mr Wood wasn't sure about doing away with the other family's bear. It all sounded a bit drastic.

"But what about his human rights?" enquired Mr Wood. "I mean, his bear rights? It would be very cruel and terrible to do something so evil to such a lovely little bear."

"That's all part of the attraction as far as I'm concerned," said Euston with a twinkle in his eye. "But consider this! If the furry little bastard mysteriously disappears you would then be left as the only person in this neighbourhood with their own small bear."

Mr Wood contemplated this for a moment.

A few moments later he was still contemplating it.

After several more moments' contemplating had gone by, Euston decided he better explain the whole thing again a bit more slowly.

Eventually the explanation somehow managed to travel deep into the dark recesses of Mr Wood's cranium and burrow its way through the thick, impenetrable shell of his walnut sized brain.

The shock of a new thought entering his little mind then caused him to leap up screeching, "Let's kill the furry little bastard like the ****ing **** he is! Ho ho ho ho ho ho ho ho!"

That was the sound of Mr Wood attempting to laugh an evil laugh but unfortunately getting it mixed up with the noise Santa Claus makes.

Downstairs someone else had also come to a similar and terrible conclusion.

"There's nothing else for it!" announced Rebecca with a small black square hanky balanced on her head. "The fuwwy little bastard must die! And when I say the fuwwy little bastard I don't mean the fuwwy little bastard in the other house. I mean the fuwwy little bastard who is living in this house with us," she added slightly losing dramatic emphasis in the process. "Euston must die!"

Rebecca's cold gaze switched between her egg whisk and a remaining shattered fragment of a stallion figurine's willy.

"Calm down now, darling!" gasped Mrs Wood. "The hospital have just phoned again. The initial results of the post mortem have been proved wrong."

"Oh weally," said Rebecca taking the black hanky off her head and reconsidering her recent threat of death on Euston.

"Yes," said Mrs Wood. "Granddad didn't die of methane inhalation after all. Smoke inhalation from the bonfire also contributed. He had also been concussed by an object falling on top of him from a great height and had somehow become infected with a very rare strain of diarrhoea that is normally only found in the very darkest parts of even darker Colombia. And by that I mean somewhere up a wild bear's arse. I wonder where on earth granddad could have picked that up from?"

Rebecca's eyes glinted coldly as she placed the black hanky back on her head.

Chapter 8

Bring Me The Head of Alfredo Bear-cia!

There was a sudden thumping at the front door. Then there was a sudden smashing, a sudden crashing, a sudden splintering and a sudden pair of figures suddenly falling through the door on top of each other. It was two policemen: Detective Inspector Alec Rankin and his somewhat coincidentally named deputy, Sergeant Alec A. Rankmore.

If these two get to the end of the chapter without becoming slightly irritated by Webecca's speech impediment it will be something of a miracle, won't it?

"Is everyone alright?" the detective asked as he picked himself up from under some shattered bits of door and his even more shattered police sergeant.

"Of course," said Mrs Wood.

"Did no-one hear us ringing the doorbell?" asked Rankin.

"Yes," said Mrs Wood.

"Did you hear us breaking the door down?" asked Sergeant Rankmore.

"Yes," said Mrs Wood.

"Well, if you heard us ringing the bell and you heard us breaking the door down," said the Detective Inspector picking bits of the smashed door off his jacket, "why didn't you come and let us in?"

"That's our housekeeper's job," explained Mrs Wood. "And Mrs Custard seems to have mysteriously gone missing in mysterious circumstances."

Inspector Rankin was already aware that Mrs Custard had gone missing some time back in Chapter 4. In fact this was exactly the reason Mrs Wood had phoned him up and asked him to come out to investigate.

"Yes, well this is all rather disturbing," continued the Inspector, "because we have recently received news from a separate source suggesting that Mrs Custard may have been the subject of a mysterious attack."

By way of proof of his allegations Sergeant Rankmore produced an invoice from Alf Perkins vacuum cleaner service engineer. The invoice detailed Mrs Custard's recent injuries and the associated repair charges including VAT.

"That is absolutely shocking," gasped Mrs Wood as she took in the horrific details and Mr Perkins' even more horrific repair charges.

"It certainly is," said Rankin, "but if it makes you feel any better we're also using the same invoice to prosecute Mr Perkins for VAT fraud."

"At least that's something," smiled Mrs Wood while inwardly telling herself, "So perish all mine enemies especially any domestic service engineers who grass me up."

"So had anyone threatened the old lady at all recently?" asked the sergeant.

"Yes!" Rebecca chipped in eagerly. "She was recently thweatened by a member of this household!"

"Now, darling, there's no need to bring your father into this," said Mrs Wood.

Rebecca responded in a very un-ladylike manner and Inspector Rankin attempted to calm her down.

"Come on, Rebecca. There's no need to get upset," said the Inspector. "Sergeant Rankmore and myself are here to help you. In fact why don't you call us by our proper names: Alec Rankin and Alec A Rankmore."

Rebecca scowled at him.

"Come on, Rebecca," said the Inspector who was clearly asking for twouble now. "I want to hear you call me Alec Rankin and my sergeant, Alec A. Rankmore."

Meanwhile, upstairs, Mr Wood was being drawn into another evil plan.

"So, Mr Wood," announced Euston grandly, "the time has come! We must do something about my wretched twin brother!"

The very thought of his wretched twin brother caused Euston's eyes to bulge out of his skull like a pair of small troublesome haemorrhoids glinting in the bright light of an operating theatre.

Euston had been driven into a frenzy by his twin brother's popularity, politeness and occasional humorous clumsiness. Now he felt he could no longer be held accountable for asking Mr Wood to go over and bump his brother off for him.

"Of course I'd love to perform the deed myself," said Euston, "but I'd be the first person the police would think to investigate. You on the other hand are a much less likely suspect."

Mr Wood wondered how his carrying out the crime would help make him a less likely suspect.

"You know I'd do just about anything for you, Euston," said Mr Wood.

Euston knew this already. Mr Wood had recently given him a long, detailed list of all the things he was prepared to do for him. It had made for several hours' rather uncomfortable reading.

"Never mind that now," said Euston, "get over there. Do your worst to the little bugger. Remember – try and keep his fur in one piece. I'm not so bothered about what happens to the middle bit."

"Yes. There's just one thing," stammered Mr Wood. "This is the one thing I don't think I can do for you."

Downstairs Rebecca had been shut out of the living room for obscene verbal abuse of two police officers.

"So, Mrs Wood," said the Inspector, "you're saying Mrs Custard had a number of enemies?"

"Can I just say in my husband's defence, Inspector…" began Mrs Wood.

"Don't listen to her! She's not telling the twuth," squealed Rebecca from outside the door.

"It's true that Mr Wood often makes murderous threats to Mrs Custard," continued Mrs Wood. "But then the old woman does quite often serve us up really burnt toast at breakfast time."

"No, you misunderstand, Mrs Wood," said Detective Inspector Rankin. "I'm talking about a particularly violent attack on the elderly housekeeper."

"Oh!" said Mrs Wood. "You must be referring to the morning we had croissants!"

"Our old housekeeper was attacked by a vicious wild animal!" called Rebecca kicking at the door. "Are you listening to me, Wankin! Wankmore!"

"Is this true?" said Sergeant Rankmore. "Are you keeping a wild animal on the premises?"

Mrs Wood made a subtle nod towards the wild shrieking creature on the other side of the living room door.

"I cannot tell a lie," she told the policemen ironically launching into a series of lies in the process.

Well, it was an opportunity too good to resist. Now at last Mrs Wood would be able to send her daughter away to be locked up somewhere until she was completely grown up.

"Our daughter Rebecca is a wild animal," Mrs Wood

whispered. "We simply can't control her. In fact we are not legally permitted to own the sort of equipment that would enable us to control her. Not only that but our domestic electricity system wouldn't be capable of carrying the required levels of voltage."

Mrs Wood presented the two policemen with such extensive evidence of her daughter's guilt that by the time Sergeant Rankmore was sent to fetch Rebecca from outside the living room door, she had disappeared.

"Bugger!" said Rankmore. "Your daughter seems to have done a runner."

"Perhaps we'd better search for Mrs Custard and make sure the poor old lady is all right," suggested Mrs Wood.

The two policemen decided this would be a poor second best to apprehending a dangerous violent juvenile.

Upstairs Euston was appalled to hear Mr Wood wasn't prepared to perform the simple act of murdering his twin brother in cold blood for him.

"You wouldn't do this one thing I asked you!" snarled Euston.

"I can't! I'm not allowed to go near that other little bear. So I can't murder him for you without breaking the terms of my restraining order," explained Mr Wood.

"You idiot!" snorted Euston. "You're completely useless! You're not capable of doing anything yourself."

"Well, we could always get the deed done the way I manage to get everything else done round here," said Mr Wood.

Rebecca stood outside the remains of the Woods' front door painting. She finished a couple of water colours and an undercoat on the door frame before realising this had been a misprint.

Rebecca stood outside the remains of the Woods' front door panting.

How could her own mother have said such terrible things about her? How could she have described her as vicious, wild and violent thought Rebecca as she flexed the specially sharpened handheld rotary egg whisk with which she intended to perform unimaginable atrocities on Euston.

Inside the house Detective Inspector Rankin peered out of the window at the smouldering remains of the bonfire in the back garden.

"Oh my God!" he exclaimed. "I think I can see something sticking out of the bottom of the bonfire."

"Ugh! It looks absolutely hideous," said his sergeant, "I think it could be the hideously decayed remains of an old lady."

"Hideously decayed you say!" said Mrs Wood. "That description fits our housekeeper Mrs Custard perfectly!"

They all rushed to the back garden. The two policemen raced ahead while Mrs Wood looked in the direction of the bonfire ashen-faced. The wind had just blown the remains of the bonfire in her direction. Mrs Wood wiped the ash off her face. She was horrified at what might they might discover.

"This is great isn't it, sir?" said Rankmore cheerfully as they pulled the remains of the hideously charred body out of the bonfire. "This morning hasn't been entirely wasted after all!"

But then the policemen's mood changed dramatically.

"Oh dear God no!" said Rankin ashen-faced. There had

just been another gust of wind. "Oh no! Oh God no! Oh dear! No oh God! Dear God! No! Dear no! Oh! Dear oh!"

"What's happened?" asked Mrs Wood rushing to their side.

"I'm very sorry to have to break this to you," the Detective Inspector told Mrs Wood, "but your housekeeper is still alive!"

"Do you want me to make a cup of tea?" said Mrs Custard pulling herself backwards out of the bonfire.

Back inside the house the blackened, battered and bruised elderly housekeeper painfully prepared a pot of tea and a plate of sandwiches for Mrs Wood and her guests.

Mrs Custard explained she had been blackening her face ready for an important mission. No-one had seen her for a few days because she had been doing a major cleaning job. She had spent the entire time clearing out the en suite toilet in the young master's room which had become blocked as a result of Euston's prodigiously productive bowels. Sergeant Rankmore put the sandwich he had just taken back on the plate.

As soon as Mrs Custard had finished that job Mr Wood had given her yet another chore. He and Euston had politely requested that she pop round to the house in the next road and assassinate the nice little bear who lived there. At first Euston had suggested that she could rely on her culinary skills to dispatch his twin brother but then Mrs Custard thought of something even better.

The old lady possessed a small incendiary device that had dropped on her during the last war and which she had kept ever since as a souvenir. So she had popped it in her shopping bag, popped out to the bonfire to blacken herself up before intending to pop round and blast the nice little bear in the next road into the middle of next week.

"Thank goodness you're safe and alive, Mrs Custard," said Mrs Wood putting on an apron so she could hug the filthy old creature.

"Yes," said Detective Inspector Rankin, "that's wonderful news!"

The policemen then slightly spoilt the moment by immediately arresting the elderly housekeeper for conspiracy to cause explosions and for blackening her face in a manner likely to cause offence to racial minorities.

As Mrs Custard was led from the house to a waiting police car, Mrs Wood raced out, took her by the hand and gave her her P45.

"Thank goodness I got to her in time," thought Mrs Wood as she waved after the police car. If Mrs Custard was still technically employed by the Woods when she was sent down for attempted murder, Mrs Wood presumed she would have to keep paying the housekeeper during her life sentence. On the plus side, she thought, Mrs Custard was quite old so it wouldn't have been for long.

Euston's plan had been foiled again. He wondered how to proceed now. He tried asking Mr Wood to introduce him to the most dangerous characters in the neighbourhood. These turned out to be a group of fifteen-year-olds who hung around outside Costcutter.

Euston tried introducing himself to them. Twenty minutes of swearing, abuse and obscenity followed after which Mr Wood was threatened and mugged at knife point. And that was just by Euston. The fifteen-year-olds had got bored and gone home ten minutes earlier.

Euston next tried checking the classified adverts in the local newspaper and the Post Office window but there didn't seem to be any killers for hire listed. If only he lived in a rougher London borough, he thought. Then there would probably be loads of adverts up.

The local butchers also said they were unable to help. Euston thought this was extremely inconsistent. They had clearly already received visits from Chicken Licken, Porky the Pig and Ermintrude the Cow looking for help in wiping out an extraordinary number of their relatives.

Euston didn't know what he could do to get his brother off the scene. The little bear looked sadly at his reflection in a plate glass window. And then it came to him. The answer was staring him in the face!

Meanwhile rough, tough local game warden Klint Van Der Klerk was in his office polishing his trophies. And that's not a euphemism. After that he polished his blunderbuss. That's not a euphemism either. After that he vigorously masturbated into a sock for five minutes. Unfortunately this was not a euphemism either. This was a point that Klint particularly regretted when he noticed that he wasn't alone after all. A figure had appeared in his office and was standing silhouetted in the doorway.

"Are you Klint Van Der Klerk?" asked a voice.

This question wasn't really necessary as the office clearly

had "Klint Van Der Klerk Local Game Warden" over the door, there was a sign on his desk that said "Klint Van Der Klerk Local Game Warden" and the individual behind the desk was wearing a badge inscribed with the legend "Hello, I'm Klint Van Der Klerk – who would you like me to shoot for you?"

"Who wants to know?" said Klint putting his khaki knee length sock back on with an unpleasant squelch.

"I need your help," said the mysterious figure walking towards the desk. "There's a small bear I need you to capture for me."

Rebecca Wood presented Klint with a small water colour she had recently completed depicting Euston suffering a savage attack with an egg whisk.

"Nice picture," said Klint, "yes, I think I know the young bear in question."

When Mr Wood opened his front door a short time later that day he couldn't believe it. The milkman had left him skimmed milk again.

But on a more positive note there was Euston, his very own small bear now dressed just as he had always dreamed – in a manner completely inappropriate to any small bear or other wild animal.

Euston was wearing a large floppy hat, a brightly coloured duffle coat and a pair of wellies. Not only that but he was wearing them all properly on the appropriate parts of his body and wasn't using any of them as receptacles in which to go to the toilet.

Mr Wood shuddered at the memory of putting his boots and hat on one morning a few days earlier and discovering Euston had filled each of them during the night.

Even more unpleasantly it had then become clear that the hat and the two boots had each been filled to the brim with a completely different bodily fluid. His wife, always one to look on the bright side, had pointed out that this represented quite an achievement for a very small bear and that it might be worth contacting the Guinness Book of Records about the matter.

Could this little bear standing before him really be Euston? Surely this was in fact the nice polite little bear who lived with the family in the next road.

"I hope you're ****ing happy now!" said the bear. "I look like a complete ****ing **** in this ****ing get up!"

No, on reflection, thought Mr Wood, it probably was Euston after all.

"Euston!" gasped Mr Wood. "You look wonderful dressed like that! You look like you're positively glowing!"

"I'm glowing with ****ing embarrassment," snarled Euston. "Now get out here and let's get in your ****ing car before anyone sees me. We've got a job to do but first we've got to pick up the other members of the gang!"

As he drove Euston up and down the dark, foreboding crescents and cul de sacs of the neighbourhood, Mr Wood felt as happy as a sand boy who has just gained access to some particularly special sand.

One by one they stepped out of the shadows. The members of Euston's gang.

There was Victoria – the skull cap and cycle cape sporting giraffe. Charing Cross – the koala in a burkha and a pac a mac. Marylebone – the hyena in the turban and parka. St Pancras – the alligator in a puffer jacket and leather flying

helmet. And Heathrow Terminal 4 – the cagoule and trilby wearing panda.

Mr Wood picked them up one by one. It was like the Magnificent Seven assembling. Except there were only six of them. Marylebone and St Pancras had just eaten Victoria.

"Could I just say," whispered Mr Wood to Euston, "you

look absolutely wonderful in your duffle coat, floppy hat and wellies."

"And could I just say," snapped Euston, "if you say that to me one more time I will personally bite off your genitals and spit them back in your stupid face. Now will you just concentrate on holding up this bank!"

Euston had indeed led Mr Wood, Charing Cross, Marylebone, St Pancras and Heathrow Terminal 4 into the magnificent banking hall of the biggest, smartest bank in the neighbourhood.

Mr Wood felt Euston had put him in an awkward position. He was holding up a bank with a bear, a panda, a koala, a hyena and an alligator.

And what's more the panda, the koala, the hyena and the alligator had all put stockings over their faces in an attempt to disguise their identities.

And Mr Wood was even more likely to be recognised because he was almost the only member of the gang tall enough to be seen over the counter.

Euston, on the other hand, didn't seem to be suffering from any such shyness. He got Mr Wood to lift him up to the counter where he announced in a loud voice that they were holding the bank up and could the cashier please put all the money in a sack and hand it to Mr Wood.

"Of course, sir. Hello, Mr Wood," said the cashier to Mr Wood.

Damn it, thought Mr Wood realising that he was also the only member of the gang who had an account at this particular branch.

"And I should warn you," warned Euston, "that if you don't hand over the money I will get this alligator, this hyena, this panda and this koala to start tearing everyone in the bank to pieces and eating them before your eyes. OK, maybe not so much the koala."

"That's right," threatened Mr Wood, "and not only that but I shall move my account elsewhere!"

It was an unusual sort of bank robbery thought Mr Wood. While the cashier started bundling piles of cash into a sack and Mr Tompkins the bank manager chatted politely to him about his ISA, Euston was walking round and round and standing in front of every security camera in the banking hall.

He stood waving in front of one of the cameras; he did a double thumbs-up to another and then did a little dance in front of a third. He even called out the bank's maintenance man to fix one of the cameras which looked like it might not be working properly.

It was almost as though the little bear wanted to be seen and recognised in his floppy hat and duffle coat. What on earth could he be up to, thought Mr Wood.

"Right! We've got the cash! Now let's run for it!" said Euston handing the cashier a large portrait photograph of himself in his floppy hat and duffle coat.

Just at that moment a shot rang out. Klint Van Der Klerk had entered the bank to make a small deposit. And it was going to be a small metallic deposit inside an evil bear.

Klint had seen and followed his quarry into the bank. Now he was thrilled to discover that not only would he bag a small bear but he would also end the afternoon with the faces of a hyena, an alligator, a panda and a koala grinning down at him from his trophy room wall.

More shots ricocheted around the banking hall. Leaflets about loans and house insurance were sent fluttering into the air. Bullets bounced off the cashpoint machines. Now the banking staff were getting upset.

"What do you think you're doing!" shouted Mr Tompkins the bank manager through a hail of bullets. "Don't you realise some of the animals you're shooting at are extremely rare?"

"And some of them are really cute!" shouted the cashier.

Klint found himself forced to the ground by a small round female financial adviser while the rest of the bank staff and other customers in the bank helped overpower him. Klint's last sight of Euston was as Mr Tompkins the bank manager held the door open to allow the gang to escape out into the afternoon sun.

Police sirens could be heard in the street outside. It was a busy day for Detective Inspector Rankin and Sergeant Rankmore.

Klint Van Der Klerk was arrested for possessing firearms and attempting to kill endangered animals. Mr Tompkins the bank manager was arrested for aiding and abetting a raid on his own bank.

Back at the Woods' house, Mr and Mrs Wood were led to a police van waiting outside. Mr Wood requested that a table cloth from the dining room be placed over his head so none of the neighbours would recognise him as he was escorted out of the house. Mr Wood had however failed to take into account the fact that the neighbours might recognise him because they knew he lived in that particular house. A lot of them were also familiar with his dreadful taste in table cloths.

Mrs Wood requested a table cloth be placed over her

head as well because, she said, she didn't want anyone recognising her as being married to Mr Wood.

Rebecca was carried out of the front door safely locked inside a straitjacket complete with Hannibal Lecter-style face mask. There were no table cloths left in the house so Rebecca's identity had to be hidden by putting a large sheet that had been decorated earlier that day with the words "Happy Birthday Rebecca Wood 18 Today" on it.

"Mmmmfffffmmmm," came a muffled sound from the under-the-stairs cupboard.

"Good Lord!" said the police inspector throwing open the cupboard door.

"Thank goodness you've come to get me out of here," cried Jocelyn, "I've been in here for weeks."

The police helped Jocelyn out of the cupboard and untied him.

"Oooh that's better," said Jocelyn, free for the first time since Euston's arrival, "I was starting to get really bad cramp just then."

"Well well well," said the Inspector looking at the piles of stolen loot that Mr Wood had attempted to hide in the cupboard with Jocelyn. "Looks like we've found the criminal mastermind behind the whole bank raid. Put the cuffs on him, lads!"

Jocelyn had been untied for all of ten seconds when he was restrained again, handcuffed and taken away to be confined in a cell at the police station roughly the same dimensions as the Woods' under-the-stairs cupboard.

"Now there's just one other member of the gang we need

to round up," said the Inspector. "The most dangerous and ruthless one of them all. Everyone be on the look out for a small bear!"

"Oh yes," said a voice behind him.

The inspector turned. A diminutive figure dressed in a grubby t-shirt and Burberry cap stood behind him.

"Ah ha!" exclaimed the sergeant eagerly. He had just noticed a mid 80s electro-pop album in Mr and Mrs Woods' CD collection.

"I wonder if you might be able to help us in our enquiries," said the Inspector to the furry miniature chav. "We're looking for a small bear."

"So many people round here are," said Euston.

The Inspector proffered a picture of a small bear in a duffle coat and wellies.

"Oh yes," said Euston solemnly examining the picture. "I know this bear very well. I always thought he was up to no good. I believe he lives in the next road."

Euston stood in the doorway and waved to the policemen as they set off to arrest the evil gang leader bear in the duffle coat and stupid hat.

"You've got a nice big house here, sir," said Inspector Rankin as he closed the front gate.

Yes, thought Euston, he would be happy here now he had the place to himself. And then just as the little bear turned back into the hallway there was a sound of screeching brakes from the road outside. Mr Wood, the table cloth still over his head, had just wandered blindly into the path of the number 121 bus service.